A Treatise on Hysterical Affections

SALZWASSER
VERLAG

George Tate

A Treatise on Hysterical Affections

Reprint of the original.

1st Edition 2023 | ISBN: 978-3-37514-402-9

Verlag (Publisher): Salzwasser Verlag GmbH, Zeilweg 44, 60439 Frankfurt, Deutschland
Vertretungsberechtigt (Authorized to represent): E. Roepke, Zeilweg 44, 60439 Frankfurt, Deutschland
Druck (Print): Books on Demand GmbH, In de Tarpen 42, 22848 Norderstedt, Deutschland

A TREATISE

ON

HYSTERICAL AFFECTIONS.

BY GEORGE TATE,

SURGEON.

THIRD EDITION, REVISED.

LONDON:

JOHN CHURCHILL, NEW BURLINGTON STREET.

1858.

PREFACE

TO THE THIRD EDITION.

SINCE the first publication of this little work, an experience of many years has afforded the opportunity of testing, upon a large scale, the somewhat original views I have maintained upon this subject, as well as the particular plan of treatment recommended.

Having committed to the press my opinions upon a professional matter of so practical a character at the early age of twenty-six, it might have been excusable if, in re-considering them at a more mature period of life, I had found much requiring modification, even if there were nothing which I might see fit to recant. Such, however, is not the case. Much might, indeed, be added by way of illustration; cases of a nature more striking and complex than those already related might be adduced, and the size of the volume extended by the introduction of new and original matter; but I can add nothing that would materially affect the principles or alter the practice propounded many years since.

In my own hands the results of that practice have been signally successful; and so many acknowledgments bearing similar testimony have reached me from various quarters, that, in preparing another edition with so little variation from the preceding one, I hope to be acquitted of an overweening confidence, as well as of carelessness or indifference.

There are, however, two points upon which I am desirous to say a few words in this preface: first, in reference to the *peculiar pain in the left side*, so common and so troublesome in Hysterical cases; and, secondly, to the *tenderness in various divisions of the spinal column:* two remarkable and very significant symptoms, which I was the first to point out, and which are now admitted to be diagnostic facts of considerable value. With regard to the former,—"pain in the left side," situated generally between two of the ribs immediately under the breast,—it has been stated by a writer of eminence that this peculiar pain does not pertain so much to Hysterical cases as to Leucorrhœa, by which it is invariably attended; the Leucorrhœa being consequent upon inflammation, if not ulceration of the uterus. At an early period of life I was so much struck by the frequent occurrence and singular locality of this pain, that I devoted great attention to it, and the train of symptoms associated with it; and experience does not justify me in agreeing with the writer in question. In a vast majority of Hysterical cases, where Leucorrhœa exists in a form more or less troublesome, there is certainly no inflammation, much less ulceration of the uterus. I express this opinion very decidedly, because there happens to be at the present time a growing disposition to adopt the opposite conclusion, which I believe to be wrong in point of fact, and most pernicious in practice; leading not only to needless apprehension on the part of the patient at a time when mental quietude is so desirable, but also to very equivocal treatment on the part of practitioners.

Though it may, perhaps, be considered rather out of place, I take this opportunity to protest against the practice too much in vogue,—I might almost say in *fashion,*—of making specular examinations of the uterus in the treatment of disorders connected with uterine irritation.

This practice, encouraged by the popularity and success of a most vicious example, is becoming daily more common; so much so, that in the consulting rooms of some practitioners it has become rather a general rule than an exceptional case. This cannot be right; and it is notorious, and acknowledged by some of the most learned and the ablest physicians, that this mode of investigation is not confined to such cases as alone can justify its adoption. All men of right feeling will admit that, unless warranted by a strong necessity, the practice is open to the gravest objection and rebuke; and knowing, as all men of experience must, the proneness of the female mind to believe in the existence of uterine disease, they should on this account, as well as from a sense of decorum, beware that their own suggestions do not excite groundless alarm, and should discountenance the practice referred to in all cases but those wherein it may be indispensable.

The other point referred to, namely, "*Spinal Irritation*," has always appeared to me to have an intimate connexion with the pain in the left side already alluded to. Dr. Ashwell, in his able and comprehensive work on the "Diseases of Women," when commenting (very liberally and kindly) upon my views and opinions on this subject, has thus expressed himself:—"After all, there is no complication more difficult to cure, even to relieve, than Hysteria, attended by *pain in the left side*. Mr. Tate has associated it with tenderness or inflammation of the spine and uterine disorder, giving the precedence to the former state." After some other observations Dr. Ashwell proceeds: "The affection of the spine, so well pointed out by this author, is not always inflammatory; frequently it does not pass the limits of excited sensibility," &c. Now in the first paragraph Dr. Ashwell has misquoted my words, and in the second has misconceived my meaning. In representing me to have said that "Spinal Irritation" precedes the uterine disturbance, he makes me utter an absurdity. I distinctly stated the reverse. I said, the *first* thing in the aggravated forms of Hysteria, about which such strange blunders are committed, is uterine disturbance, and the *second* Spinal Irritation; and thence are all the fantastic phases of this multiplex disorder disseminated.

In the latter paragraph Dr. Ashwell appears to have been under the impression that I consider the spinal tenderness to depend on inflammation; whereas it will be seen in the following pages that, instead of giving countenance to such an opinion, I have altogether discarded it.

A man of Dr. Ashwell's acuteness should not have made such a mistake. It should have been apparent that if, in allusion to spinal tenderness and irritation, I had meant to inculcate the presence of inflammation of the spinal sheath, or ligaments, or bones, I should have stood convicted of leading into dangerous error, where it was my purpose to enlighten and instruct. Whether the mistake of Dr. Ashwell be attributable to deficiency of clearness on my part, or to his cursory mode of reading, it is not for me to say; but, in publishing a new edition of this work, it became necessary to correct a misrepresentation involving an entire perversion of sense, and placing principles and remedies in direct antagonism.

While reiterating what I wrote upon these disorders many years ago, I must express my regret that we have not been able to proceed further, showing the means by which the uterine disturbance and spinal irritation are connected together, and tracing through each link in the physiological chain the varied mimetic affections that are engrafted upon them. Both Dr. Ashwell and Dr. Marshall Hall have found themselves in a similar difficulty; and, therefore, as regards my own want of success, I need not complain. Having, through a not very short life, watched with much interest the distinguishing characteristics of the Hysterical state, sometimes so important to the prevention of most disastrous mistakes, I was in hope that further observation would not only sanction what I had written upon these affections, but would have led to an elucidation of the mysteries in which they are involved, and have explained them so as to satisfy the fastidious scrutiny of science. Up to this time, however, the keenest research has been baffled in the inquiry; and even those who have done so much for the removal of physiological darkness in other fields have failed to throw much additional light upon this.

We know the source, we witness the effects, and we can administer to them with tolerable success; but why from the same cause the effect is so various, and the change so sudden—why the hysteric patient laughs one moment like a maniac, and weeps the next—why she pants with the force and quickness of a hunted animal one hour, and the next you cannot perceive her to breathe at all—why she loses for a time her voice, her hearing, her sight—why first one side becomes paralysed, then the other, then the whole external surface void of feeling—why the highest state of sensibility is aroused, to be succeeded by a deathlike stillness—why every vital function is in turn inverted, or for a time suspended altogether—these things we see, but we cannot explain. They seldom endanger life—often vanish like phantoms; but frequently imperil the reputation of medical men, and put their sagacity to a very severe trial.

It is to be hoped that we may yet penetrate much that now appears dark, and that all these things, which "overcome us like a summer's cloud, and excite our special wonder," may at no distant time be removed from the field of speculation, and made consistent with a sound philosophy.

65, Camden Road Villas, N.W.,
September, 1858.

A

TREATISE ON HYSTERICAL AFFECTIONS.

CHAPTER I.

It fell to my lot at the age of twenty-two to have almost the sole charge of an extensive country practice; and although I came down from the Hospitals, as I fondly believed, brimful of information, prepared to compass every case that might present itself, I soon discovered that neither books, nor Lectures, nor Hospitals, had made me quite the practical man I had vainly imagined.

True, I did not fall into the error of mistaking muscular pain in the side for pleurisy, nor every disturbance of the heart's action for organic disease; but some extraordinary cases of an hysterical character stupefied and confounded me, at the same time very seriously deranging my self-complacency. Indeed, an incredible number of cases of simulated disease crossed my path at this early period of my professional career. I sought in consultations with older men a relief from my own bewildering doubts and cares; but in vain. They could throw little light upon the deep obscure. Hysteria may well be called—

> "An Ignis Fatuus that bewitches,
> And leads men into pools and ditches."

For the old gentlemen fell into as many quagmires as myself. Baffled and dissatisfied, I was compelled to think for myself, and determined, if possible, to discover some general distinctive marks that would stamp the character of hysterical disorders, and enable us to base the treatment on more rational and certain principles.

The following pages disclose the results of my studies. It is surprising that in the whole mass of medical literature no attempt has been successfully made to unmask these affections, and dispel the clouds that envelope their more complicated forms. This omission does not arise from the paucity of writers; for the field of medical literature has of late years swarmed with labourers; but it has been the custom, from time immemorial, to consider the early stages and common forms of Hysteria with either ridicule or severity, as being made up of nervousness, fancifulness, and imbecility, and altogether undeserving of serious attention.

Then, again, with the exception of those common forms which are popularly called "Hysterics," the symptoms are so various and indefinite, that they could hardly be classed under the same general name: besides which the pathological conditions have been very little understood; and the multifarious shapes it assumes are so curious and extravagant as almost to defy description or even belief. Hence it has too often happened that the health of the patient and the reputation of the practitioner have both been shipwrecked together.

It will not be expected that I should be able to divest the subject of all perplexity, or to clear away the darkness in which it has been hitherto involved. I do not hope to be so far successful; but my design is to separate, if possible, such facts as are authenticated by my own observation and practice, from the undigested mass of fiction and error with which they have been so long combined; to relate, in a clear and rational manner, what I conceive to be the causes, the appearances, and (what is of the highest consequence) the distinguishing characteristics of these affections; and, afterwards, to describe the plan of treatment which appears most proper for their cure.

As was before remarked, this class of disorders has been regarded as of insignificant consequence, and of brief duration; but that is a mistaken idea; for, if overlooked or treated ignorantly, they are as painful in their progress, as tedious in duration, and productive of as much misery as any disease in the medical vocabulary.

And here I must venture to say, that although Hysteria in some of its forms may be under the best management tedious and harassing, I believe its remote effects upon the delicate females who are most liable to its invasion, may with more justice be imputed to medical treatment than to the unassisted agency of the disorder itself; and that many of its unhappy subjects, who might have obtained almost immediate relief, have, in consequence of carelessness, ignorance, or rashness, been abandoned to all the horrors of a protracted sickness and of a shattered constitution. So many cases in confirmation of this have fallen within my own observation, that, however severe the remark may appear, it is certainly just; and no subject demands more discriminative talent, more skill and care, than the class of disorders I am considering.

The late Dr. James Johnson, with whom I frequently corresponded, first encouraged me to publish the result of my observations on this subject; and it is hoped that, if the work is not altogether satisfactory, it will at least give many persons a more correct notion of Hysteria than they at present entertain, and enable those who have had little or no experience of its varieties, to recognise them when they occur in practice, to administer to them with confidence, and at the same time save them from the disgrace of making their remedies worse than the disease. Hysteria is, in some of its shapes, most embarrassing; and those who are aware of this will not despise any light that may be cast upon it, but will appreciate, *first*, the importance of obtaining such a knowledge of its forms as shall enable their real nature to be at once ascertained, and distinguished from other diseases which they frequently imitate; and, *secondly*, the importance of knowing the appliances and means that are best adapted for their removal. Without such knowledge, no man can be safely armed with confidence in his measures, or with patience to follow one course, perseveringly, for any useful length of time; and it is for want of this knowledge that young practitioners are daily inflicting irreparable mischief by the adoption of wild, furious, and unsuitable measures, which are only calculated to break up the health of their patients, and poison the future enjoyment of their lives.

It would be an unprofitable waste of time to enter here into a history of the barbarous notions which the old physicians entertained of Hysteria. These are now obsolete, or nearly so; and, but for the circumstance that thousands must have suffered martyrdom under their treatment, might afford some diversion, but would be otherwise useless.

CHAPTER II.

ON THE CAUSE OF HYSTERIA.

WITH the exception of those cases, real or affected, which are so frequently occurring in what have been called "the refined circles," occasioned sometimes by sudden impulse, and sometimes by mere caprice, Hysteria, in all its varieties, whether it be mild, yielding to a brisk cathartic,—whether it be of another form, lasting for weeks,—or whether it be more obstinate, persisting for months, or even years,—has one common cause which is essential to its appearance; namely, an irregular or defective menstruation. Since I have been attentive to cases of Hysteric disorder, I have never seen one, (with the above unimportant exceptions,) either of a simple or of a complex character, in which this state of things did not co-exist. There is always some deficiency or some depravity of this secretion: it will be found sometimes altogether suspended; sometimes redundant, or too frequent in its recurrence; but perhaps more often attended with great pain and sickness. Sometimes, also, Hysteria will take place at puberty as the harbinger and indicator of that interesting period; and it also will often occur at a later time of life, when another important change is about taking place in the system.

Seeing, then, that Hysterical cases, in their

strange and endless varieties, whether called "Hysteria," or "Catalepsy," or "Proteian Malady," or "a peculiar spasmodic affection," or "Leaping Ague," or any other fanciful name by which they have been distinguished, are never produced, unless one or other of these conditions prevails, it is clear that this is its fundamental cause, and that our remedial means ought to be directed to that cause more attentively than has been the practice hitherto.

This view of the subject is at variance with that entertained by many; but it has, at least, been founded on a multitude of facts, to some of which I shall, by and by, advert. It has been supposed, not only that the state of the uterine functions has no share in the production of Hysteria, but that men are liable to its attacks. It would be presumptuous to deny the fact; but if I substantiate the correctness of my own position, by the narration of a series of facts, and by reasoning upon them, it is impossible to admit that men can, under any circumstances, be amenable to a disorder, the very elements of which are confined to the opposite sex. It is more probable, that those cases which have been called Hysteria in men, were really Chorea, or other affections, as many cases occurring in females have been called Chorea and other things, which, as will be shown hereafter, were really Hysterical.

Debility produced by, or at least combined with, a deranged state of the stomach, liver, and bowels, certainly predisposes to Hystreia; and delicate females, who are easily excited, are more susceptible of it than the robust; but there is still something wanting to account for the singular phenomena that this affection exhibits. These phenomena are different from those presented by any other disease: they are perpetually changing their character,—adopting the image of the most terrific maladies,—and are scarcely ever seen in two cases precisely alike. The cases to be afterwards adduced will, I think, prove conclusively uterine irritation to be accountable in the first instance for that disturbance in the equilibrium of the nervous system through which so much distress is engendered.

Many cases are herein described as Hysterical to which other writers would have applied different names; but looking at their common origin, and at the organs which are principally concerned in their production, I have, for simplicity's sake, classed them all under one common term, as there is no other distinction between them than such as proceeds from their different degrees of violence or duration; and as the word "Hysteria" expresses the intrinsic nature of the disorder, it is a more fitting term than any other, and less likely to lead to confusion or mistake. It is, however, necessary, for the purpose of description, to make some sub-division of the subject; and the most simple will be to call them Hysteria of the first degree, Hysteria of the second degree, and Hysteria of the third degree; but even this distinction is hardly practicable.

CHAPTER III.

HYSTERIA OF THE FIRST DEGREE.

It is hardly necessary to enter into a tedious history of the common form of Hysteria. It occurs, like other forms of Hysteria in females, almost invariably between the ages of thirteen and forty-five. It is always attended with some irregular menstruation, and the stomach, liver, and bowels (one or all) are generally out of order. It is characterized by alternate fits of laughing and weeping, starting and screaming, lying still as death, and struggling with gigantic strength. Generally, there is a loud rumbling in the bowels, called Clangor Intestinorum, and the Globus Hystericus, as it is called, causing a sensation like that of a solid ball rising in the throat and producing a sense of suffocation. There is often an accompanying copious secretion of pale urine; but this is rather incident to a confirmed hysterical habit, than to an occasional sudden explosion such as we are now considering.

For the cure of this kind of Hysteria, the most offensive drugs used to be considered specifics; and some of these are not to be altogether dispensed with in those simple cases which are seen distinctly to arise from some mental emotion, and where the animal functions are only thereby secondarily disturbed. But, at the same time, I must protest against the idea of such means being really useful, except in such a case as this; for Hysterical attacks are invariably connected with bodily disorders, and will set at defiance all the stimulants and antispasmodics in the universe; during which time the patient is suffering incredible distress, for want of a little judicious treatment, such as would dispel all signs of the attack in a day, or even in a few hours.

The first object, in the treatment of this form of disorder, is to cleanse the bowels; and this is most effectively done by a brisk dose of calomel and jalap. In a great majority of cases, a smart action upon the bowels will be attended with immediate relief of the fits or paroxysms, and they will rarely return if the subsequent practice be judicious: which consists merely in avoiding stimulants; in living on a bland and nutritive diet, and taking aloetic aperients, with or without preparations of iron according to circumstances, until the uterine and alvine secretions are properly regulated. It has frequently happened, in the course of my practice, that after having relieved a young girl from the immediate attack, I have represented to her mother the necessity of repairing the deranged state of her general health; and those who have been for years feeble and out of condition, going about with sallow and sickly faces, parched and pallid lips, furred tongues, and limbs incapable of the least exertion, have been indebted to a few doses of calomel and jalap, followed by preparations of aloes and iron, for the perfect re-establishment of their strength, health, and beauty.

Then, in cases of common Hysteria, occasioned by mental excitement, and nothing more, to which there never can be much difficulty in tracing them, such stimulants as Ammonia and Valerian may afford relief; but in other circumstances,—where the fits are not manifestly referable to such causes, but where, on the contrary, they recur frequently, and the general health and uterine secretion are found to be deranged,—the same treatment is not appropriate; it will not effect a cure, nor even palliate such symptoms as may seem to be urgent.

CHAPTER IV.

OF HYSTERIA OF THE SECOND DEGREE.

This is of much more serious consequence than the foregoing form, is infinitely more insidious, and more likely to lead to a misapprehension of its real nature, from the variety of shapes it may assume, and the number of formidable diseases it may resemble. Hence it has obtained the cognomen, "Protean Malady;" which is an unmeaning name, as not being expressive of any pathological condition,—as giving no clue to its nature, and no guide to its treatment. It is, in fact, a mere mask for ignorance, and, in the present advancing state of medical science, ought to be altogether abolished.

This form generally arises, like the preceding, rather suddenly, with some singular and unaccountable symptom, very alarming to the patient's friends, and a medical man is hastily summoned to her relief. If he be not upon his guard, he will be very apt to mistake this disorder for some real disease or some active internal inflammation. He may thus do more mischief than all his subsequent treatment can repair.

Before saying anything of its symptoms, or varieties, I shall relate some cases illustrative of this affection, which will show how strange and alarming they must appear to an inexperienced person, and prove the necessity of obtaining such ample information as will enable a man always to detect their real nature, and, in the midst of a confused and terrified family, calmly to assure them of a patient's perfect security, and of her speedy recovery.

Case 1.

A. W., aged 19, a rosy-cheeked, healthy-looking country girl, came to me early in the morning of the 22nd of April, 1825, complaining of violent pain in her eyes, which seemed inflamed, and discharged a copious flow of scalding tears. The intolerance of light was extreme. This had come on without previous shivering or other warning, a few hours before she left home, and she could assign no cause for her illness. The conjunctiva was about as much injected as it is generally after a violent fit of crying. She was immediately bled from the arm; and after losing about eight ounces of blood, she opened her eyes, and declared she could see as well, and bear as much light, as ever she could in her life. The pain, also, was nearly gone; and this without any fainting or any perceptible tendency to it. She was then ordered to go home, to keep quiet, and to live low for a day or two; calomel and jalap, with sulphate of magnesia, were also prescribed for her. At about four o'clock on the following morning, I was called up to go to her immediately, (six miles into the country,) as the people about her declared she must die, unless she could obtain instant relief. I found her seemingly in agonies. Her eyes continued well; but she was breathing with such excessive rapidity as I can only compare with that of a hound after a hard run, and with much the same kind of muscular distress. Her hand was pressed firmly against her left side, beneath the breast, where her gestures (for she could not speak) signified that she was suffering acute pain. It was impossible to ascertain the state of her pulse, in consequence of the agitated state of the respiratory system, to say nothing of her terror; but her chest sounded well, and she was in a profuse perspiration, attended with high heat of the whole surface of the body. Upon inquiry, I found that she had not menstruated for fourteen weeks, and for more than twelve months very inadequately to her former habits; and had complained of pain in her left side, with occasional palpitations. These circumstances shed some light upon the rather puzzling appearances of the case, and went a great way to determine its real source and character. I then had her turned round, to get an examination of the spinal column. On making pressure upon the four uppermost dorsal vertebræ, she complained of great tenderness and pain. As I had always found these, or some other divisions of the spine, tender, on the application of pressure, in urgent cases of Hysteria, I was quite satisfied that this was nothing more than a mysterious case of that description. The fugitive nature of the apparent ophthalmia, the seat and kind of pain in the left side, the pain in the dorsal vertebræ, with a suspended menstruation, all concurred in giving it this and no other character. Although not expecting much benefit from it, at the solicitation of friends, she was again bled, with scarcely any relief. The treatment which I chiefly relied upon was the tartar emetic ointment to the spine. This was applied along the whole course of the dorsal vertebræ, three times a day; and she took calomel and cathartic extract, followed by an aloetic mixture.

In the course of that day, and the following night, many dark and offensive evacuations were procured; after which, the breathing and lateral pain were somewhat relieved. On the 24th, her pulse was 120. Tongue brownly furred. The eruption had not yet appeared. Leeches were applied to the side, and the other medicines continued. On the 25th, the eruption was visible in considerable quantity. Her breathing became nearly natural, and the pain in the side very much diminished. She could now talk composedly, and was free from all appearance of distress. On the following day, her only complaint was that of the pain caused by an antimonial plaster, which had been removed in the night, having elicited a sufficient crop of pustules. The pain under the left breast was gone, her breathing and pulse were natural, and her tongue clean.

From this time she was gradually recovering her health and strength; but continued to take the aloetic mixture, with iron. The Catamenia, however, did not appear, and at the end of six weeks she was attacked in a precisely similar way:

the side being again painful, the respiration again rapid, and the spine again tender. The same treatment was adopted, and she soon recovered.

It would be well to observe, that, in consequence of her great repugnance to a re-application of the ointment, a blister was, in this second attack, placed over the course of the vertebral pain, but without removing or even mitigating it in the smallest degree: and this fact tallies with the general result that has attended blistering, as a substitute for the tartar emetic, in these cases. No sooner, however, did the pustules appear, than the pain and other symptoms immediately yielded. There still remained some tenderness in the spine; to dispel which, a third application of the ointment was requisite. Afterwards, under the constant use of aloetics, she menstruated; and since has enjoyed uninterrupted good health.

The case just described was evidently Hysterical, resembling first ophthalmia and afterwards symptoms of acute inflammation. It will be noticed that pressure upon the first four dorsal vertebræ occasioned pain; and that there was pain also underneath the left breast. To these points, at present, I merely direct attention; as I shall notice them more in detail, after the relation of some other cases.

Case 2.

Miss W., aged 15, was taken ill at a boarding school. For a few days she had complained of head-ache, and loss of appetite; and, without any further warning, awoke on Sunday morning, after a tranquil night, with a train of symptoms resembling Tetanus. Her governess sent to me in great alarm. The following was pretty nearly her condition when I first saw her: she was lying upon her head and her heels, her back being thrown into an arch, and scarcely touching the bed-clothes. Her arms were flexed and rotated inwards; her fingers violently closed, grasping her thumbs, which were stuck into the palms, in a way that is seen in hydrocephalic children, called the carpal spasm. Her toes were bent inwards, and her legs bent and twisted in the same manner as her arms. It was with great difficulty that the hands could be forced open, although the attempt did not much annoy her. She was perfectly sensible, and complained of violent heat and pain in the head. There was great intolerance of light; and when her eyelids were opened, she squinted frightfully. The breathing was short, and she complained of pain in the side, and palpitation. Her pulse was 110; her tongue clean, skin hot, but covered with moisture; she was thirsty, and her mouth was dry. Her general health had been previously good. *She had never menstruated.* Such was the striking appearance of the case; which, from the suddenness of the attack, after passing a good night, and from her having never menstruated, with the corresponding symptoms, I strongly suspected was nothing more than a strange form of Hysteria. Under this impression, I examined the spine; and the moment pressure was applied between the scapulæ, upon the upper dorsal vertebræ, the patient complained of pain, which was also manifested in the shrinking expression of her countenance. That which was conjecture before, then became matter of certainty; and I felt myself warranted in assuring the governess, who was naturally in considerable alarm, that these formidable symptoms were mere phantoms, which would readily disappear; and that a few days would, probably, be sufficient to restore her to her usual good health. The infrication of the tartar emetic was immediately begun throughout the dorsal region; and calomel and jalap were prescribed for her. As soon as the bowels were freely evacuated, her head was better, and respiration was relieved; but the spasmodic, or rather, tetanic affection did not yield at all. In about thirty-six hours, the antimonial ointment had accomplished its duty; when the spasm was immediately influenced, the flexors gradually relaxed, and, in less than twenty-four hours after the pustulation was developed, not a vestige of the disorder remained. The contractions returned twice or thrice, to a partial extent, in the course of the following month; sometimes one thumb, and at another time one or two fingers, being bound down; and, upon one occasion, this lasted for several days; when a second application of the ointment was, very reluctantly, consented to. She had, afterwards, no return of pain or disorder. During the whole of this time, aloetics, with iron, were daily administered; and, at the expiration of five weeks from the accession of her illness, she menstruated; and was afterwards quite well. Thus proving, very satisfactorily, that the amenorrhœa was the source of the vertebral irritation; and that this, in its turn, produced the other ailments.

Case 3.

Miss L., aged 19, had not been in good health for nearly four years before the date of the present seizure. When first called to her, she had been ill several days with most acute pain in the left side, which was increased on inspiration, but relieved by pressure. This was so violent as frequently to make her scream, and beg her friends to hold her sides; which was often done for hours together. There was considerable pectoral oppression, and her head was in much pain. A few hours before I saw her, she had fallen suddenly back in her chair, apparently lifeless; and was carried to bed. In this state she would lie for half an hour or an hour; recovering at intervals, and speaking rationally and even cheerfully, and then again suddenly sinking into a state of perfect coma. While thus seemingly comatose, her breathing would be suspended for ten minutes, or longer, at a time; or carried on with so much subtleness, that no air escaped her lips;—no rising or falling of the chest;—no motion of any muscle, except a quivering of the eyelids, could be detected to show that she was not actually in a state of syncope. Then a rapid gasping would follow, succeeded by another deathlike stillness. Her eyes were then turned up, her teeth fixed, her hands convulsively clenched,—so that nothing could relax them. Now, during all this while, her pulse was perfectly regular and quiet; except that she had occasional palpitations of extreme violence, which shook her from head to foot, and continued through her illness. The little colour she usually had, did not forsake her lip and cheek. When, for a few minutes, she recovered, she always made great complaint of her side, head, and chest; and she could not endure the least exposure to light without pain. She entreated me to leech her, which I did; as she assured me the pain in her side, which she had suffered the last four years, had always been relieved by bleeding. Having never seen this young lady before, on hearing a description of her sufferings, and that she had been in delicate health for so long a period, it occurred to me that there was some disease of the heart, to which all her symptoms might be tributary: and it was not until after I had seen her in one of her comatose attacks, that I took a correct view of the subject, and became satisfied that this was one of those anomalous cases of Hysteria, the phenomena of which cannot be satisfactorily accounted for,—which are only to be seen in females, and in them only under particular circumstances. Having convinced myself that there was no real disease of any organ, either of the head or chest, and that the various animal functions, except that of menstruation, were properly conducted; I proceeded to examine the spine from the upper to the lower part; and, throughout the dorsal portions, pressure produced uneasiness, making her shrink from the fingers; upon increasing the pressure, the pain was increased, and passed through to the pit of the stomach, and to the left side, at the spot so long complained of. It caused the breathing to be oppressed. There was also some tenderness in the cervical vertebræ. In making particular inquiry into the state of the Catamenia, I found that they had appeared a few days before the attack, and were unusually scanty and dingy: at that time, I did not think a trifling irregularity of that kind sufficient to cause the development of such remarkable symptoms. Even at the end of several days, the least exertion, the mere effort of swallowing any mild fluid, threw her into a state of coma; in which she acknowledged that she was sensible of all that was passing around her, but was quite incapable of speaking, or of voluntary motion.

Upon the discovery of the pain, and tenderness of the spine, the antimonial ointment was rubbed pretty freely into the back; and, upon the eruption coming out, it was astonishing to see how immediately the symptoms vanished. The fits went off, the head and side were no longer complained of, and the palpitation gradually subsided. Upon the disappearance of the pustules, she had one or two slight returns of the attack, particularly of the pain under the left breast; but they were soon dissipated, and she began to regain her health. It is now four years since her recovery; and, with the exception of an illness she had, of a different kind, about two years ago, she has enjoyed much better health than she had for years before, but is certainly not robust. Indeed, I have known her, upon many occasions, when in moderate health, fall suddenly back in her chair, apparently without sense or motion. In the course of half an hour or sooner, after having thrown the company into confusion, she has recovered; making no complaint of pain, and being as cheerful as others. I have had suspicions of the young lady's sincerity upon some occasions; at all events, the fit frequently came on, as a lady once complained to me that her ague did, "at very unseasonable hours."

Case 4.

Elizabeth M., aged 20. Early one morning, I was sent for to this young woman, and found her in bed, where seven or eight persons were employed in keeping her by main force. She had complained for some days of a bad head-ache; was of a pale, delicate complexion, of a very slender frame, and had been for many months without any uterine evacuation. She had waked in the night, screaming out like a maniac, to the terror of all the family; and, in attempting to get out of bed, had fallen back in a state of insensibility, and had continued so up to the time of my arrival. She was struggling with amazing violence; her eyes were staring wildly, she was grinding her teeth, her hands clenched, and every muscle of the body seemed to be thrown into a state of most tremendous spasm. This was Hysteria, clearly enough. So far there was little difficulty in deciding. Her pulse being rapid and bounding, some blood was drawn, but without affording her the smallest relief. Calomel and jalap were, with some difficulty, forced into the stomach. When these had copiously relieved the bowels, she became calm, and the convulsive throes ceased; but the insensibility was unabated, and she lay like a girl perfectly dead, till the middle of the following day. I had already begun the tartar emetic inunction; and when she was sufficiently sensible to answer, I traced the course of the spine, and she complained and shrunk away when the fingers were applied upon the dorsal vertebræ. The pain was felt through the whole chest, particularly at a spot beneath the left breast. Indeed, I have scarcely met with a case in which the spinal affection was more strongly and clearly marked. Besides the tenderness of the spine, and the pain in the left side, there was, in this case, excessive tenderness in the right side, under the margin of the ribs; this was so great, that she dreaded the slightest manual examination, even before she was touched. The pain was confined to the hepatic region, but was too acute and too superficial to induce a suspicion that it was connected with visceral disease. It was, as well as that of the other side, occasioned by the spinal disorder; and as soon as this was relieved by the usual application of the ointment, and the uterine functions were restored by a combination of iron with aloes, these pains were dispersed, and the young woman afterwards acquired greater strength and better general health than she remembers to have enjoyed at any former period of her life. This, as I before remarked, has been the usual result of Hysterical cases, treated in the manner above described.

Case 5.

The following may, perhaps, be called a simple case; but it is important, as showing the inefficiency of the usual modes of relief, and the powers of the tartar emetic ointment.

Miss L., an unusually stout and healthy girl, had been, for a few weeks, in bad health; complaining of pain in the left side, and occasional palpitations. She was seized with fits, which her parents fancied (as they generally do in these cases) must be fatal to her. There was no laughing, crying, nor violent gesticulation; but she had convulsions of the whole body, lasting sometimes for hours together, which were of a choreal character. During the fits she had no power of utterance, and was insensible to everything. In the intervals, she complained of intolerance of light and of noise; pain down both the arms, palpitation, pain under the left breast, distressing head-ache, with great heat of its surface, and Dyspnœa. These, with the Globus, which was very troublesome, made up the train of her symptoms. This was the usual period of menstruation, which, for many months, although regular as regards the intervals, had been attended with severe pain in the loins; and the discharge was of a dark and depraved character. Such was the case at this time, and was apparently the cause of the present attack. In the course of the first three days after the attack took place, she was leeched in the temples, and blistered; active aperients were given her, with ammonia, valerian, and other antispasmodics; but without effect. The least movement excited the fits; as, for instance, the act of raising her in bed, or swallowing a drop of fluid. As soon as she became sensible to feeling, I made pressure upon the vertebræ, at the part I have repeatedly stated to be particularly affected in these cases; and she winced under the touch. In any other part, the finger might be applied, with a moderate degree of pressure, without giving pain; but having once felt that produced by pressing the upper dorsal processes, she would not suffer them to be touched again. This was a case like the last, in which the spinal tenderness was extreme. I again called in the aid of the tartar emetic, with the usual success; assuring the parents that, as soon as the eruption should make its appearance, the fits would vanish altogether. In the mean time, as her head suffered very much, more leeches were placed upon the temples, and it was bathed constantly with spirit and water; in attending to which, the ointment was neglected till the following day. Three days more elapsed, therefore, before the eruption was complete; during which interval, no impression was made upon the disorder by other means, but the patient had no return of the paroxysms afterwards.

I have thus traced the leading features of five cases of what I would call Hysteria of the second degree. These are enough to show that it is sometimes wrapped up in such forms, and may put on the mask of so many other diseases, that great nicety and care are occasionally requisite for its detection. An intelligible description of a disorder of so chequered and varied a character, is attended with much, if not with insuperable, difficulty. Yet there are fortunately in Hysteria, whatever shape it may assume, and by whatever name it may be called, some distinguishing characteristics which admit of being clearly stated; and by which it may be recognised almost with as much facility and certainty, as if its form were invariably the same. By attending to these leading symptoms, and disregarding the curiosities of particular cases, the practitioner will rarely feel himself at a loss to know the nature of the disorder when it presents itself, to give it at once its simple name, and to apply his equally simple remedies with equal assurance of success.

These distinguishing marks were present, more or less, in all the preceding cases; and I now proceed to point them out in detail.

CHAPTER V.

SYMPTOMS OF HYSTERIA OF THE SECOND DEGREE.

I. In the first place, menstruation is defective. It always is, and has generally been some months prior to the attack, in some respect, more or less deranged. This derangement is the "head and front" of the case; the original cause of the disorder; that upon which all the other symptoms are more or less dependent.

II. The next circumstance, and the most important of all, whether as regards the discrimination of the disorder, or its treatment, is this:— that, in every case, there is distinct pain upon the application of pressure or of heat to three or four of the six superior dorsal vertebræ. This is a point upon which I desire to fix the reader's attention; for this spinal affection, whatever its intrinsic quality, is clearly chargeable with most of the curious images and fantastic forms that Hysteria is accustomed to put on; and yet, notwithstanding its constant occurrence in these forms of Hysteria, and its frequent existence where there is even a *tendency* to Hysteric disorder, it is a circumstance that has been overlooked by those who have professed to treat upon the subject, as well as by those who, for the sake of gratifying curiosity, have published detached cases of Hysteria under various other designations.

In other parts of the spine, especially in the lumbar vertebræ, pain is frequently complained of for a long time; but, in the dorsal divisions, no uneasiness is generally felt until pressure is applied. Indeed, if the patient be asked if she have pain between the shoulders, she will usually answer, "No!" and will think it very troublesome to be disturbed for the purpose of exposing the part to examination. Proceeding from the uppermost cervical vertebræ gradually downward, she will smile at the inquiry, "if the pressure of the fingers hurts her?" until the dorsal vertebræ are reached; when her countenance will immediately betray her, and she will shrink from the touch, confessing that the pressure causes a pain which frequently, but not always, goes through either to the chest or to the left side, sometimes to both, and generally oppressing the breath.

It is not to be understood that this pain is always present to the same extent: sometimes the vertebræ are extremely tender, even upon the lightest pressure, or the least heat; and, at other times, they bear a moderate degree of both, without much suffering; but the pain is invariably present in greater or less force, bearing some proportion generally to the violence of the Hysterical manifestations: and leaving an aching or soreness in the part for some time after the fingers have been removed.

I do not wish to suggest any hypothesis that I may have "dreamed of in my philosophy," respecting the abnormal condition of portions of the spinal cord affected in Hysteria, but only to state facts that are practically useful; leaving the exploration of hidden causes to those who have more time and opportunities for it. No case that I have seen, either of this or of the extreme form of Hysteria, to be afterwards considered, has terminated fatally; so that it is impossible to say, with any certainty, what is the state of the spinal marrow and of its membranes in these affections; but it may be fearlessly asserted that no severe or protracted case of Hysteria ever occurs, in which this pain is not perceptible, when heat or pressure is applied over the spot; and there is no doubt that, by a more extended investigation, all the fallacious symptoms and sensations that beset patients in the anomalous forms of Hysteria, will be proved to arise from a high state of excitement of the upper dorsal portion of the spinal marrow, which, through the ganglionic system, has some connexion with the due discharge of the uterine function. Whether this excitement be merely irritation, or whether it consist of something more, I will not pretend to determine.

III. Another thing to be attended to, as a diagnostic system, is pain in the left side. This is very peculiar. It is usually situated immediately below the left breast, in a hollow formed between the cartilages of the fifth and sixth, or sixth and seventh ribs; it is generally so circumscribed, that it may be covered by a shilling; and is of the gnawing kind. Occasionally, however, it is most acute, feeling as if a knife were being stuck into the spot, and the patient cannot forbear screaming. This pain is complained of for some time before the invasion of the Hysteria. The patient is often observed to incline the upper part of the body to that side, dropping the left shoulder, which relaxes the painful part and affords some relief. The act of raising the left arm above the head, or of bringing the body into a perfectly erect position, is attended with an increase of pain. I apprehend this pain is really seated in the intercostal nerve, although I have sometimes thought it must be situated in the nerves of the heart itself; as it is difficult to account for its perpetual preference for the left side. The right side, certainly, is often not exempt from pain; but, in nineteen cases out of twenty, the prominent grievance is in the former; and in the like proportion of instances you can put a finger on the spot with as much certainty as if it were visibly marked.

It is highly probable that many spinal curvatures have arisen solely in consequence of this pain, which is often of very long standing, causing a tendency to lean the body constantly out of the perpendicular line, towards the affected side. In these cases, nothing is more easy than to mistake the effect for the cause. When, therefore, other symptoms supervene, and a medical man is called in, he must not immediately determine the curvature to be the cause of the patient's illness, as it will frequently turn out to be merely the consequence of another disorder. I have seen a young lady confined to her bed for nearly three years by this very mistake; and nothing was gained by it, but an increase of weakness.

IV. Palpitation is another symptom that is almost universally present, and is often distressingly violent and tumultuous.

Now, in addition to the uterine disturbance, I have enumerated three prominent symptoms which accompany severe and aggravated Hysterical attacks, viz., the spinal pain or tenderness, the pain in the left side, and the heart symptoms. These are very important, and require profound attention, because each, taken separately, might lead to the belief in structural disease. Take the heart for example. In these Hysterical cases, the heart's action is sometimes not merely violent, but entangled with other signs and stethoscopic sounds, usually associated with organic disease, so that the closest vigilance and circumspection are required for the prevention of mistakes. The most eminent physicians have fallen into such errors. I knew a young lady who was confined to her bed and sofa for four years, and condemned by two celebrated Physicians * to die of diseased heart, when she was perfectly free from all disease and from all danger. At length, being suddenly seized with an hysterical attack, which her friends

* One of these was the late lamented Dr. Hope: the other being still extant, and in practice, I cannot disclose his name; but, should any one doubt the fact I am relating, I shall be happy to give him access to the family in question, so that he may have his doubts removed or satisfied.

supposed to be the crisis of her fate, a local Surgeon was called in to administer relief. Having subdued the immediate attack, and quieted the alarm of the family, he fortunately detected the true character of the symptoms that had led the learned physicians astray; and, under proper treatment, in the course of a few weeks, the young lady was perfectly well. About a twelvemonth after this lucky fit of Hysterics, which was the accidental cause of her escape from an imprisonment worse than penal servitude, she was married, and had not a trace of organic disease of the heart, for which she had been so long and ceaselessly confined to her bed, nor of any other organ.

In another case, where the Heart symptoms were very urgent, a Physician of high provincial celebrity used these remarkable words:—"There is not a *single organ* sound and healthy within the chest; all are diseased." Yet, in truth, as the event proved, there was no *single organ* in the slightest degree impaired, but only suffering from disturbed and perverted action consequent upon the Hysterical state, and the excited condition of the ganglionic system of nerves.

Mistakes such as these are really deplorable. They compromise the peace and comfort of whole families for years together, if not for life. If, at last, the error is rectified, there is no redress for all the misery that has been endured by the victim of such discreditable mistakes, nor for the needless anxiety and expense incurred by her friends. Allowance should be made for inexperience; but when men of reputation, and of high professional rank, whether from want of care or want of penetration, fall into such injurious blunders, I know no words of censure too heavy to denounce them.

Again, the tenderness in the course of the Dorsal Vertebræ, in the absence of ancillary symptoms, would lead to hesitation and doubts; but, taken in conjunction with the others I have mentioned, there need be no mystery or confusion. How many girls have been thrown upon their backs unnecessarily for years, in such cases, under the suspicion of diseased spine, only the records of the dead can disclose; but I have no doubt that they may be reckoned by hundreds! The late Mr. Segar, of Cheltenham, had a young lady under his care, whom he condemned to the recumbent posture for nearly three years, and from whom he received more than seven hundred guineas in fees, till, growing tired of the unchanging tediousness of the case, her brother consulted another medical man, and, within a month afterwards, she was promenading the walks of that delightful town in perfect health.

The third point specially alluded to, was pain in the left side. By the observing practitioner, this pain would perhaps be regarded in its true light; but not so with those of less tact and experience. In the hands of such men, sad havoc is generally made of a constitution already enfeebled, and a further prostration of strength is often the result of a treatment based on the belief in the existence of inflammatory action or structural injury.

There is another feature in Hysterical cases which is often embarrassing to men in early life. This is an acute tenderness over the surface of the abdomen, which is constantly mistaken for peritoneal inflammation, leading to the application of a crowd of leeches, followed by blisters and other active remedies. After the lapse of many days or weeks of this treatment, all the symptoms are aggravated. The pulse is quicker, the pain more extensively diffused, and no relief in any respect secured. By this time possibly the practitioner may begin to suspect that he has been mistaken in the nature of the disorder; that, instead of a case of peritoneal inflammation, he is dealing with a case of great nervous excitement arising from Uterine Irritation. He will bethink himself that the abdominal tenderness and pain on pressure are far more acute than ever is the case in real inflammation; that, instead of a very obstinate state of the bowels, as in inflammation of the membranous covering, they are rather relaxed and irritable; that the urinary secretion is undiminished and natural; that the fever is not high, nor the thirst great; that there is no change in the respiratory organs; and that the features are not marked by great distress. Now, by taking these things into account, in the first instance, with other circumstances before mentioned, the unhappy error of regarding such *cases as inflammatory* need never occur. A soothing plan of treatment will succeed in putting matters to rights. Persistent fomentation of the abdomen, mild and nourishing diet, together with Ammonia, Henbane, and Quinine, will do more good for the patient than "*shoals*" of leeches, which are now talked of as glibly as if the perpetual drain from them were an amusement that might be indulged at all times, and under any circumstances, if not with advantage, at least with safety; but experience teaches otherwise. The loss of blood from a crowd of leeches often occasions not only a great decrease of muscular power, but a still more serious blow to the nervous system: and those who have had much to do with cases of nervous exhaustion, know full well what a work of time and labour it is to restore the balance of power in that mysterious and subtle system.

Besides the other symptoms, there is always pain in the head, in front or in the occiput, or in both; intolerance of light, which is sometimes so extremely urgent that the patient is easy only in absolute darkness, and generally more or less globus.

Such are the special symptoms which denote Hysterical cases of this class: a suspended, irregular, or painful menstruation, pain upon pressure upon some of the dorsal vertebræ, pain underneath the left breast, palpitation or fluttering at the heart, more or less intense pain in the head, intolerance of light, and more or less globus. These *are always* combined in every case; and, in the great majority, are accompanied by pain or aching in the arms or legs, and across the loins, furred tongue, constipated bowels, and excessive flatulence. The pulse is a delusive guide, being sometimes quick, variable, or intermitting; at other times perfectly natural.

Difficult, then, as it is to recognise some cases of Hysteria, when surrounded with a host of extravagant symptoms, the practitioner can hardly fail to come to a right conclusion, if he will carefully institute an examination of the matters alluded to. When he finds these symptoms concurring in a case, no matter how puzzling or grotesque its other features, he may be at once satisfied of its real nature; and that being clearly known, all embarrassment ceases, and the mode of treatment is not difficult, and will very rarely fail of success.

CHAPTER VI.

TREATMENT OF HYSTERIA OF THE SECOND DEGREE.

It has been already stated that the various forms of this kind of Hysteria, however monstrous and unaccountable, appear to be caused *immediately* by the spinal affection; which is, in its turn, the result of some occult association or sympathy between the contents of the upper dorsal portion of the spinal canal, and uterine irritation. There are thus two points in the treatment to be separately considered. The first, the removal of the immediate cause of the Hysterical evolutions; the second, the restoration of the uterine and other secretions to a state of health and vigour. The most speedy and successful mode of accomplishing these views, is that pointed out in the cases herein described.

I. In some instances, where the patient is very robust, the cheeks highly flushed, the eye injected, the forehead red and polished, it may be allowable to abstract blood; but it rarely does much good, nor does it relieve the immediate attack. But when symptoms so sudden and alarming make their appearance, a medical man is expected to do something *instanter;* and, in strong young women, bleeding does no harm. In delicate girls, on the contrary, it aggravates the disease tenfold; *and renders* the cure infinitely more difficult and tedious than it would otherwise be. As a general rule, even in the most urgent cases, the application of a few leeches is alone required.

Having made a careful examination of the spine, and ascertained the seat of pain, the first thing to be done is to apply the tartar emetic by friction on the part. If the symptoms be urgent, —whether cataleptic, or choreiform, or tetanic, or hemiplegiac, or any other,—the application should be carried throughout the whole course of the vertebræ; and this should be done every six or seven hours, until the pustulation is fully developed. The Hysterical symptoms will then begin to yield, and the patient will become calm and sensible: but as the cause of the spinal disorder, viz., the faulty uterine function, is still in operation, it is sometimes necessary to establish the eruption a second time, in order to secure the patient from a recurrence of the same symptoms. In the mean time, every exertion must be used to improve the condition of the uterine organs.

Upon the discovery of this tenderness between the scapulæ, I have frequently leeched the part, which has generally failed to afford important relief; I have afterwards blistered the spine, without deriving therefrom, at best, more than partial benefit; but the antimonial eruption exerted always a most powerful influence over the disorder; controlling its various manifestations, relaxing muscular contractions, and dispelling the tenderness upon pressure, and the pain on the application of heat.

It must be presumed, that the action of this pustular eruption is attributable to counter-irritation; but it is singular that it should be followed by such decided effect, after leeches, blisters, cupping, and the like, had failed to produce any influence over these disorders. However, such is the fact, and its *methodus operandi* is of minor consideration.* It ought, however, to be remembered, that the ointment is extended over a much larger surface than that occupied by a blister, which may account for its more manifest effect.

In addition to this, it will be necessary to give the patient aperients, more or less active, to clear the whole course of the intestinal canal. Calomel and Colocynth, if the patient is robust, generally effect this purpose in the best manner. The evacuations are generally of a very black and unhealthy appearance; the medicine must be repeated at intervals, according to the discretion of the practitioner and the strength of the patient, until the secretions become natural.

Objections have been urged against the use of calomel in these affections; and it must be remembered, that where there has been for a long

* In further proof of the value of this application, I will just relate the following striking case. Some years ago I was asked to visit a poor woman who had been confined to her bed for several months with Paraplegia. She had been under the care of a surgeon, who had told her she might take what she pleased, as he had given her up as incurable. I examined the lower part of the spine, and found that there was pain in the lumbar vertebræ; here I ordered the tartarized antimony to be rubbed in; a crop of pustules was the consequence. In less than a week afterwards she was able to walk, and she got rapidly well.

period, as often happens, a pale and sickly countenance, with a languid expression, tumid and spongy gums, a clammy and tremulous tongue, with red edges, and a tainted breath, calomel should be very cautiously employed; but in patients, and they are many, having no apparent debility or laxity of fibre, there can be no danger in using it, and no other aperient medicine is of equal efficacy.

II. We have thus disposed of the immediate attack; but another important indication in the treatment remains to be considered. This is to re-establish a healthy menstruation. Now the mal-performance of this important function may be of several different kinds: it may consist in absolute suspension or suppression; in being later or more frequent than usual; in being of a dark or of a very pale and watery character; in being unnaturally excessive, or small in quantity; or in being attended with unaccustomed suffering. Such being the various states of disorder, it will be seen how impossible it is to lay down any rule of treatment that can be universally applicable. Each must be separately considered, and treated according to the discretion of the practitioner, upon the usual principles; in first of all improving the secretions, and placing the digestive organs in a healthy state. After this has been effected, wholesome air, wholesome food, and wholesome exercise, with preparations of iron, and the use of the warm, tepid, cold, or shower bath, according to circumstances, will generally be the best tonics, and restore *the patient to her* usual health and strength.

CHAPTER VII.

In further elucidation of the correctness of my view of this class of Hysterical affections, and of the value of the treatment recommended in their varying circumstances, I propose now to transcribe, as briefly as possible, some remarkable cases that have been recorded by different practitioners, and called by equally remarkable names. These cases will prove to have been merely examples of Hysteria, though their reporters appear, generally, to have entertained rather a confused notion of their nature, and not a very clear one of their treatment.

The following case is called *Catalepsy*. It is related by MM. Legarde and Lenormand; and was seen by Loennec and Recamier.

Case 6.

"Mademoiselle —— first menstruated at the age of 15. She had previously enjoyed good health. *She had only menstruated thrice, and stopped.* She went to school at Paris in June, and pined to return to her parents. In November she had fever, and recovered in three weeks, afterwards obstinate constipation and difficulty of taking food. Purgatives had little effect in moving the bowels. Symptoms of Chorea now appeared. *The head,* arms, and legs were in constant motion.

She had deep-seated pain in the chest, especially under the sternum. In January the Choreiform symptoms diminished, and were succeeded by Trismus and permanent contraction of the muscles of deglutition. During eight days only a few drops of fluid could be got down her throat. A few days after these phenomena she became affected with Cataleptic symptoms: complete immobility, rigidity of the whole body, eyelids shut and fixed, eyes turned up, pupils natural, pulse feeble, total abolition of the senses, except that of hearing. She heard what passed around her, but could make no answer or sign. On recovering from these states she complained of violent pain under the sternum. She tried to soothe her parents, and endeavoured to swallow. Cold affusions and other things were tried with little or no effect. In the third week of the Cataleptic and Trismal attack, some changes took place. She could no longer hear; but her limbs became moveable, and retained any position in which they were placed. *Thus the disease was now complete Catalepsy.* These attacks were, for some days, strictly periodical; lasting from four till half-past ten P.M. In the interim, there was pain and anguish about the stomach, greatly augmented by taking food. On January the 14th she went home to her parents, but the Catalepsy still came on at the same hour. Various means were tried to dispel the attack, but they only protracted the patient's sufferings. She had now been ill nine weeks. On the 27th of *January, during* the Catalepsy, she was seized with convulsive movements: the arms were suddenly thrust out of bed. The countenance expressed great suffering. Her eyes suddenly opened, and turned convulsively upwards; the lower jaw descended, and closed alternately; she frothed at the mouth, and began to sing. In the night the choreal affection of the head returned; it ceased, but returned on the 28th and 29th. During the succeeding days a kind of somnambulism took place: she sung several airs, talked aloud, and went through several movements during the Cataleptic period; which was, however, shortened, and was followed by complete oblivion of all that had passed during its continuance. *An antimonial plaster was applied to the stomach,* causing dreadful sufferings for eight or ten days; but having no influence upon the disorder. By the 15th of February she was completely exhausted; she could scarcely speak, was indifferent to everything, and took hardly any nourishment. The Cataleptic accession was now ushered in by a sense of excessive coldness, but the real temperature of the skin was not changed. From the 19th of February to the 10th of March the Catalepsy so much increased, that there were very short intervals between the paroxysms. She might be moulded, like a figure of wax, to any shape, and would remain in that form till altered to another. She was extremely emaciated by want of food; went two or three weeks without an alvine evacuation; fæces unnatural. About *this time,* Recamier and Loennec thought the young lady dissembled, as, when she thought herself alone, she could move her hands freely; but when any one was near, she was Cataleptic from head to foot. From the 13th of March the Catalepsy daily declined, and she began to take food, move, speak, laugh, &c. The paroxysms were now slight, but periodical to the moment, till the 30th of March. She gained flesh, and was tolerably cheerful. · Except a few *nervous and anomalous attacks*, she gradually got well; and on the 4th of May left Paris convalescent. *The menses had not re-appeared.*"

That this case was of the Hysterical kind, from first to last, no experienced man will doubt. Notwithstanding the suspicions of the Doctors, that the young lady was duping them, it is quite certain that the suppression of the menses was alone sufficient, through the uterine connexion with the spinal and great sympathetic nerves, to occasion all the phenomena that here exhibited themselves; both the singular hallucinations of mind, and the fantastic muscular contortions. Had the spinal column been attentively examined, pain and tenderness would have been found to exist there; and if the tartar emetic plaster had been applied there, instead of at the epigastrium, this young lady would have been speedily emancipated from her sufferings; and would not have lingered on for four months, being reduced to the last extremity of misery and weakness. We see that, at last, she *recovered* by the mere force of her natural strength. *Menstruation did* not, however, take place; and, unless this were brought about, (as probably it was, when she again enjoyed the country air, and the privilege of making a free use of her limbs,) it is not unlikely that she may have relapsed into a similar state: if so, perhaps she may now be languishing away her life as an incurable invalid; which has been the case with many young ladies in this country, under parallel circumstances.

Case 7.

The following case occurred in the Middlesex Hospital, and the Report is headed "*Chorea fatal.*"

"E. Smith, aged 17, was admitted under the care of Dr. Hawkins, on the 5th of September. She had just recovered from a severe attack of rheumatism in her knees and shoulders, which lasted seven weeks. A fortnight before her reception, she was seized with involuntary convulsive movements in the legs, arms, and neck. These had continued ever since with great violence. *The catamenia had been suppressed four months.* She had had head-ache, thirst, pain in her back, pulse 96, tongue loaded, bowels constipated. She was actively purged, without success. The calomel, senna, and turpentine, always dislodged dark and copious motions; but produced no alleviation of the convulsive spasms, which were like those of hydrophobia. She could not hold her head quiet for an instant, and the grinding of her teeth was so violent, as to force one of them from its socket. The convulsions were uninterrupted, except by *short intervals* of broken sleep. Her intellects were unimpaired. She was put into a warm bath, which aggravated her convulsions, produced great irritation, and inflammatory symptoms. Sixteen ounces of blood were drawn; it was *inflamed.* She was bled again the next day,—still very little alleviation of the spasms. Musk was then tried without effect. Camphor and opium procured her some sleep: after taking them the second time, she slept soundly; awoke, and soon afterwards expired, on the 13th of September; being eight days after her admittance.

"*Dissection.*—No morbid appearance could be found in the brain. There were tubercles in the lungs, and earthy concretions in various parts. Adhesions between the liver and adjacent parts; intestines healthy in appearance; omentum and mesentery studded with numerous cysts; some containing a black, semifluid matter, others calcareous depositions. Several large concretions in the pancreas. *The uterus was rather large and vascular, and the lining membrane of its body and fundus highly injected. The Fallopian tubes and ovaries contained a good deal of the black matter above-mentioned.*" Dr. Hawkins says, that "granting irritation of the brain and nervous system to be the proximate cause of Chorea, sufficient cause for such irritation was met with in the preceding case;" namely, the earthy concretions. The reviewer adds: "We cannot accord in this opinion, as the earthy concretions must have existed for *many* months previously, without being productive of *any irritation.*"

It is quite clear that the earthy concretions were as innocent of the girl's death as the man in the moon. But let us take another view of the subject. We have "the catamenia suppressed four months,"—"the uterus enlarged and vascular,"—"the lining membrane of its body and fundus highly injected,"—"the Fallopian tubes and ovaries filled with a quantity of black semifluid matter;"—and are these no causes of irritation? Now it appears to me, that the whole uterine system was in a high state of vascular excitement; and that this, instead of being a case of Chorea, was in reality a case of Hysteria; and I have no doubt, that had an examination of the spine been instituted, the pain and tenderness, so often insisted upon by me, as a very important feature in these cases, would have been here immediately detected. The catamenia had been suppressed four months. The convulsions came on a fortnight before her admission to the hospital; and for seven weeks previously she had been suffering from a violent attack of rheumatism in her shoulders and knees; making nine weeks in all. It thus seems that the rheumatic affection came on seven weeks, or thereabouts, after the last appearance of the menses; consequently, three weeks after the proper period of their return. Judging of the case from this report of it, it is very probable that the rheumatism itself was of an Hysterical kind. *That* gave way, and the convulsive motions supervened. These were tremendous; and their violence, it *may be presumed*, produced the patient's death.

Whether a timely application of counter-irritation to the spine would have rescued this unhappy girl from an early death, it is hard to say. The dissection shows her to have been in extremely delicate health; and, therefore, in a more excitable state; more liable to the invasion of spasmodic disorder, and less able to cope with its violence.

The reviewer, in concluding a few remarks upon the case, says: "We question whether this disease was entitled to the name of *Chorea*;—was it not more properly convulsions?" It was, no doubt, convulsions; Hysterical convulsions; and their violence, in her weak condition, destroyed the patient.

Case 8.

The following is recorded by Dr. Fountain, of New York, and is given very briefly, having been merely reported to show the immense quantity of arsenic that was given the patient. It is called "*Chorea*." The patient was a girl 14 years old, of very sanguineous temperament, but delicate constitution, who had previously enjoyed good health, and menstruated regularly for some time.

"*The Catamenia became suppressed in July*. Dr. Mead gave her tonics till the 13th of the following September. On that day she first showed symptoms of Chorea, and Dr. Fountain was called in. He advised an emetic, to be followed by bark, and steel, and aloes, and myrrh, and assafœtida. *On the* 21st she was worse in all respects;—*pulse 95; tongue* clean; strength declining;

spasms 'frightfully increased;' articulation and deglutition difficult;—mind alienated;—violent screaming;—hair dishevelled; 'in short, exhibiting the most melancholy and heart-rending picture that can be imagined.' Dr. F. now gave her ten drops of arsenical solution every two hours, and, by the 25th, she had taken three hundred drops. 'By this time the vascular action had become intense,' the pulse quickened to 120 in the minute, the spasms considerably abated, and the patient enjoyed some sleep. She now took arsenic pills for a change. On the 26th the spasms ceased entirely."

This was clearly another case of Hysteria, which was cured by the substitution of another disease; as the reporter says, "the nervous irritation having been supplanted by vascular action." The catamenia were suppressed in July; on the 13th of September the spasms began; in thirteen days afterwards they ceased, or were driven away. The remedy, however, carried to such an extent, was of rather a desperate kind; and few will be disposed to imitate such treatment. All the symptoms would have been dissipated in three days after their accession, by the use of the antimoniated ointment to the spine; where pain would, no doubt, have been discovered to exist, as in other cases of the kind.

The following is called "Mr. North's Case of Catalepsy;" and Mr. North very properly applies the term "Hysterical" to it.

Case 9.

"The patient was, as usual," says the report, "a young female, who came to London in a state of great mental inquietude, resulting from a love affair. First, she had pain and swelling in one foot, then intense pain in the head, with slight hysterical paroxysms, &c.; in short, each day presented a new form of disease, which so puzzled her medical man (not Mr. Smith) that he thought the devil was in the girl! A physician was consulted, who pronounced the complaint Hysteria. When Mr. Smith was called in, the girl was supposed to be dying. She was apparently in a profound sleep, into which she had fallen after a violent attack of Hysteria. No motion could be perceived in any part of her body; no pulse in any artery; scarcely any action of the heart; no respiration; pupils contracted; temperature of the body below par. She drew in a gentle and deep inspiration about every ten minutes. A stimulating enema, *and four drops of croton oil on the tongue.* She continued in this state twelve hours, when a slight hysterical paroxysm dissolved the spell. After an interval of a few days, there was a violent trembling of the whole body, succeeded by a short sleep, and then an attack of Hysteria. In a day or two afterwards the real Cataleptic phenomena were developed. 'She resembled a figure of wax which might be moulded to any form. In whatever position she was placed, she remained as immovable as a statue, however awkward and fatiguing it might be. She was put

sioned by their sympathy with some cause of irritation in the uterine organs: and, although the report is silent upon the subject, there can be little doubt that menstruation was either totally suppressed, or manifestly deranged; and that some of the dorsal vertebræ would have been found, upon pressure, distinctly, if not extremely, tender. That the application so repeatedly referred to, would have been successfully employed, and that it would, in one week, have scattered every vestige of Hysteria, is pretty certain. As it was, let us see what course the case took. The unfortunate girl had, first of all, to undergo the varied discipline of three different practitioners. How long she was subjected to this, we are not informed; but it must have been for many weeks, at least, and without any remission of symptoms. She was then conveyed to St. George's, where she was treated with the same want of success. How long she remained here, also, does not appear. The last thing we hear is, "She is now in the country, still suffering from violent attacks of Hysteria." So that this patient was successively under the treatment of three medical men before she entered the Hospital, and, perhaps, of as many more within its walls; and, at last, she appears to have been dismissed the house, if not incurable, at least uncured.

This is a case, the history of which reflects little credit upon the science of medicine: it shows that *there must* be something radically wrong in the *notions entertained* upon the subject, when we see a disorder, known and recognised as Hysteria, baffle the skill and ingenuity of five or six different practitioners of reputation. But I believe, that if the points before urged upon the reader's attention be carefully marked, and if the antimoniated plaster be vigorously used in combination with other remedies that have been mentioned, such an opprobrium, as this case certainly must be considered, need never recur.

Case 10.

This was a case of Chorea, occurring in a girl nine years of age. I introduce it merely to show that the tartar emetic ointment was successful, after ordinary means had failed. The case was treated in the South London Dispensary. The complaint began in January, in the form of slight convulsive movements in both sides of the body. These were always increased by mental despondency. She had occasional headache, and diarrhœa. Her brother was subject to epilepsy. She had now the usual symptoms of Chorea, but not in a severe degree. Purgation was assiduously employed, and leeches applied to the head: but a month's treatment on this plan merely aggravated the convulsive movements. Ether, valerian, and opium, were now conjoined with the purgatives, but still she grew worse. She could now scarcely stand or walk. The head was ordered to be shaved, and the tartar emetic ointment to be applied, which brought out a copious crop of pustules. The convulsive movements on one side now subsided. The pustulation was extended to the spine, and with beneficial effects. The bowels were kept open by calomel and jalap: she ultimately but slowly recovered.

There could not be desired a clearer instance of the salutary effects of the antimonial eruption than this. Supposing the same period to have been consumed in the second set of remedies, as in the first, two months would have been thus lost, in pouring all sorts of things into the little patient's throat: but the disorder resisted every effort to put it down, until the ointment was applied to the head and spine. It then yielded, and would have done so two months before, had the ointment been put in earlier operation. I would just remark here, that, in the present case, it was hardly justifiable to pustulate the head; as this is attended, usually, with very much suffering, and is only requisite in cases of great inveteracy. An application limited to the upper part of the spine, would have answered the purpose here, just as well as a more extended punishment.

The reviewer says, "The cure is to be attributed to the counter-irritation upon the head and spine;" —but I doubt if the counter-irritation produced by blistering would have been equally availing. It is difficult to understand precisely the principle upon which the tartar emetic eruption proceeds.

CASE 11.

THE following is a very striking case of Hysteria. It is called "A case of strange and anomalous nervous Symptoms in a Female; imitating organic Diseases, and disappearing on the Eruption of the Catamenia."—Elizabeth Babillon, aged 37, a widow, entered La Charité on the 14th of May. She was the mother of five children; had been healthy, regular, and strong, till mental afflictions disturbed her health, and even her reason. For this last derangement she had been some time in the Salpetrière. When received into La Charité, she complained of *violent palpitations,—tightness across the chest,—pain in the left side*;—symptoms which she attributed to a fall she had had some eighteen months before, when she was in the habit of being bled every two months. The pulse was irregular and intermittent; beating of the heart, heard over a considerable space;—no œdema. The patient was considered highly nervous by M. Fouquier; was bled, leeched, and placed on very rigid regimen. The cardiac symptoms speedily abated; but now the patient had violent pain in the head, chiefly over the right side, which was relieved by the application of cold water. Whenever the head was relieved, she felt pain and stiffness in her limbs. In a short time there was complete paralysis of the right side, both of sensation and motion. Acupuncture on that side excited no sensation. Sinapisms,—blisters. In the beginning of September, the right leg, hitherto paralysed, became completely rigid, and remained permanently extended. When flexion was forced, great pain was produced. Both thumbs were, at this time, rigidly extended; and there was little sensibility in either arm. M. Andral now succeeded M. Fouquier, and applied moxas to the loins, which restored sensibility to the legs. But now there was intense pain in the region of the heart, "*radiating*" thence along the left arm. No fever, —no convulsions. Next day (11th September) a sense of constriction was felt in the throat; deglutition was difficult, and the voice nearly extinct. After some other metamorphoses, *we find the menses appearing, on the* 15*th of September, when the whole of these teasing phenomena vanished like a dream.*

In this case the first symptoms,—pain in the left side, palpitation, pain and tightness across the chest,—taken in conjunction with the suspended menstruation, were sufficient characteristics to have led to a suspicion of their nature, and a consequent examination of the spinal column; and here would have been discovered another collateral fact to stamp the case as Hysteria with almost absolute certainty. The patient was under the care of MM. Fouquier and Andral, from the 14th of May to the 15th of September. In the course of these months she was bled, leeched, acupunctuated,—sinapisms were applied, blisters were applied,—and, at last, moxas to the loins, in addition to the usual quantity of medicinal libations: *all which* things were heroically performed without any precise view, either of the cause, or of the condition, upon which the symptoms depended; and, at last, Nature, as if in ridicule of the punishment that had been inflicted upon this poor woman, returned of her own accord into the usual channel; for we find the menses appearing, and the symptoms vanish. This case bears irrefragable testimony to the source from whence all these phenomena spring, and to the injurious tendency and folly of such a violent mode of treatment.

Case 12.

This case was published by Dr. Fallot of Namur, and is called "Periodical Contraction of the lower Extremities, after Suppression of the Menses."

A strong country girl was pursued by a dog during the catamenia, *which were suddenly suppressed.* This was in May. In December she consulted Dr. Fallot; there being no return of the uterine discharge, although leeches innumerable were applied to the Labia, &c., and warm bath used. In September she began to feel a sense of formication in her legs, attended with painful twitchings, which no effort of the will could prevent. In October, they amounted to convulsive contractions of the legs, by which the heels were drawn up to the hips; and any attempt to stretch out the legs produced severe pain. This state of rigid contraction lasted five days, and then ceased. A month afterwards the same phenomena returned, lasted four or five days, and then vanished. The patient seemed, in other respects, in perfect health;

plump, ruddy, and strong. Dr. Fallot now conceived that the complaint depended upon *periodical congestion of the vessels of the spinal marrow, and its membranes;* and ordered sixty leeches to the *lower part* of the spine. The flow of blood was abundant; but three days afterwards, the contraction returned, though not in a violent degree. The leeches were several times reiterated in the course of the ensuing month, and the contractions returned no more. The menses did not re-appear till the following March.

This was another variety of Hysteria, arising from a similar cause, which would have yielded to the same treatment as the others. The shoals of leeches appear to have answered the same purpose; but, be it remembered, the bleeding by sixty leeches, several times repeated, is not always a sacrifice that can be ventured upon with safety. Dr. Fallot thinks the periodical contraction was occasioned by congestion of the spinal marrow, and its membranes. This is purely hypothetical. All we know is, that there is a species of Hysteria arising from suppressed menstruation, with which the symptoms usually denoting spinal irritation are very frequently associated.

Case 13.

The following belongs to the same class as the foregoing, and is extremely interesting, as well as curious. It is related in Dr. Burrows's work on *Insanity.* It is called "A Case of Catalepsy, *combined with* Mania."

"A young female of some education, after having lived in concubinage, had the offer of marriage, provided it took place the very day after the proposal. Her agitation of mind brought on a sudden eruption of the menses; and, in this state, the marriage was solemnized. The newly-married couple set off in the evening, in a stage-coach, to the place where they were to sleep. After sleeping an hour, she suddenly awoke in violent alarm, saying she had had a frightful dream, and complained of dreadful pain in her head. Presently she jumped out of bed, and flew to the window, which her husband prevented her from opening; she then became unconscious of all around her, and fainted. On recovering, she was delirious and furious. The catamenia ceased from this time. The practitioner who attended bled, purged, blistered, leeched, bathed, and starved the patient; and, in about three weeks, the symptoms gradually abated. A visit from her husband and some friends produced a relapse; and mania, in a mild form, supervened. This changed to melancholia. A fortnight afterwards she was removed to Dr. B.'s establishment. Her countenance was sullen and pallid; eyes heavy, turgid, and cast down; tongue foul; bowels inert; pulse rather full, and slow; skin, particularly of the extremities, below the natural heat. She was averse from moving or speaking; made frequent pressure on her head; and the carotid arteries beat stronger than any others. Sinciput hotter than natural,—*extremities* colder. The head was shaved, and cold lotions applied; occiput cupped; purgatives and emetics given her. This was the 10th of November. On the 24th some ptyalism came on from calomel, and all the symptoms were better. On the 8th of December, ptyalism ceased, and the bad symptoms returned. On the 18th she assumed the cataleptic character; preserving the exact posture, whether lying, sitting, or standing, in which she is placed; eats mechanically whatever is put into her mouth: if spoken to sharply, the only notice is a sardonic grin. The skin is like wax, and colder than natural; feet very cold; pulse feeble; respiration scarcely perceptible; eyes fixed and turned upwards; evacuations natural; sleeps well, and in the morning is dressed, like a helpless infant. On the 1st of January all the symptoms aggravated; sensation and volition quite suspended; evacuations involuntary; sardonic expression; mouth open, and constant flow of saliva; eyes immovable, and imbedded in the upper eyelids; every limb retained the position in which it was placed, the most painful being sustained without suffering, and for a longer time than would be possible in health. Pinching and pricking did not arouse her. These paroxysms lasted through the day. She now exercised but one voluntary animal function, deglutition. Various remedies, including depletion from the head and spine, were used without effect.

"On the 12th of February, she awoke in possession of every faculty, corporeal and mental; assisted in domestic affairs, and talked rationally.

The next day she was again torpid and mute. She was now cupped and vomited, and a seton was put in her neck. At this period she was removed from Dr. B.'s asylum; but she derived great benefit from the seton; the menses re-appeared, and she perfectly recovered."

Dr. B. says, "Many circumstanccs in this case indicated determination of blood to the brain;" and names the interruption to menstruation as one of these. This idea appears to be altogether supposititious, and not the result of philosophical induction from facts. There is not a single unequivocal sign of determination of blood to the head mentioned; and as to the suppressed menstruation being such, this must be either a misprint, or a woful proof of the shifts to which men will resort for the support of a favourite hypothesis. There is a tendency in the mind of every thinking man, upon observing a certain effect, to search for a cause sufficient to its production. Now the judgment is often less vigilant than the imagination; and, this being extremely ingenious and sanguine, the former is easily overmatched: hence it follows that where the cause, of which one has been in pursuit, is enveloped in much mystery, one is frequently led to the reception of unsound opinions, and to reason upon them with as much confidence as if they were irrefragably correct, rather than give the matter up without arriving at any settled conclusion, and having only his labour for his pains. This was the case with *some ancient* philosophers of the natural as well as of the medical world; and, in modern times, we have seen the unsubstantial theories of both demolished and ridiculed by men vastly inferior to themselves both in genius and knowledge.

That the suppressed menstruation, together with its premature discharge, was the cause of the various evolutions that this case presented, is written upon the very face of it. The suppression was contemporary with the onset of the attack, and the ailments ceased when the menses reappeared. In fact, it is quite clear that this was nothing more or less than an ungovernable case of Hysteria, and that the patient had no more business to be locked up in a lunatic asylum than Dr. Burrows himself. It is not stated that any examination of the spine was made, by pressure or otherwise: had this been done, Dr. B. would have been at once satisfied of the real seat of irritation, and such discovery would have led to a more speedy deliverance from the disorder, than was effected by the treatment pursued. As it was, we see that no material impression was made upon the case until after the seton was introduced, and that *then* the patient gradually recovered. It is by no means a novelty to find these disorders associated with maniacal symptoms; and, indeed, in cases wherein the head is so universally painful, it would be surprising if it did not sometimes happen. This was the only circumstance of the case upon which any doubt can arise. That determination of blood to the head was not the cause of this young woman's complaint may be inferred for the following reasons. We do not find determination of blood to the brain causing such effects in men, or in the absence of such an exciting cause as is here alluded to; neither do we see it suddenly sinking down, of its own accord, to a just equilibrium for a day, leaving the patient perfectly free from disorder, and "assisting in domestic affairs," and the next morning becoming as violent as ever. Besides, after bleeding, blistering, cupping, leeching, bathing, purging, and vomiting had failed to afford relief, it was hardly to be expected that so intractable a case of determination of blood to the brain would have so quickly yielded to the quiet operation of a seton in the nape of the neck. But this is not the first time that "determination of blood to the head" has been made a scape-goat in obscure diseases. It is a very plausible and convenient term, because people are apt to think they know the meaning of it very distinctly; but, perhaps, no medical term is more abused or more unmeaning than this "determination."

Case 14.

The following case is recorded by Mr. Crichton in the "Edinburgh Review." It is called "*Leaping Ague.*"

"In January, 1818, the author was called to a brisk and lively girl of fifteen. In October, 1816, thieves broke into the house. She sprang out of bed, leaped out of the window, and roused the people of the adjoining house. This shock was *followed* by another, the death of a sister. She became pensive and *bewildered,* was affected with excessive perspirations, and her strength gradually declined. At one period, in the summer, *the catamenia made a slight appearance, but never returned.* Towards the close of 1817 she had frequent attacks of shaking, followed by coma, which, after continuing about an hour, gradually went off. At the beginning of 1818 the case assumed the following appearances. Every morning, about ten o'clock, she became torpid and drowsy; about eleven, she began to arouse; by twelve she got out of bed, went about collecting her trinkets and other things she had secreted the previous day in holes and bye places. These she brought to bed, and amused herself with for some time; occasionally conversing with those in the room, but in such language as was difficult to understand; commencing her sentences with the last word, and frequently pronouncing the words themselves with the last letter foremost. When she could not make herself understood, she would write what she wished to convey; but, in doing this, she would begin at the right edge of the paper, and write backwards; the last word of the sentences, and the last letter of the words, often first: this was done with rapidity, and seemingly without consideration. Her sight also was affected, seeing objects only in certain situations, and being obliged to turn her head in another direction when she wanted to view anything. About one o'clock, she again secreted her trinkets, &c., and began dancing the Copenhagen jig. Her excitations increasing, she jumped upon the tables and chairs; sometimes running round and round the edge of a table with great velocity, then springing up and squatting herself upon the top of the door, swinging backwards and forwards without any hold, and often manifesting a desire to spring out of the window. Upon one occasion, the door being open, she suddenly sprung out, clearing the staircase at one bound, and without sustaining any injury. The strength of several people was insufficient to keep her in bed, as she got away from them like an eel. About two o'clock, becoming exhausted, she went to bed, fell into a deep sleep, awoke in her right mind, and quite unconscious of all that had passed. She continued so till the next morning, when the same scene was re-acted. Various medicines were used with little effect; but the disease gradually subsided, and a voyage to the Baltic completely restored the young lady's health."

Such was the strange, eventful history of the case, which had nothing of ague about it; but was, as the Reviewer observes, "one of those indescribable forms of Hysteria, which defy all systems of nosology, all doctrines of pathology, and, too often, all kinds of remedy, except time."

I have thus given a brief rescript of eight cases, related by their several reporters under such name as each individual has arbitrarily fixed upon, apart from any systematic arrangement, and seemingly without having recognised the cause or *condition* from which they sprung.

They appear, indeed, to have been published rather as curious specimens of the wild and extravagant vagaries of nature, than as subjects fit for serious reflection; no attempt being made to trace them to their source, or to found upon them any useful principle or method of treatment. To no one of them is there appended an account of a successful treatment, or any guidance in similar occurrences. I have brought them together for the purpose of proving that these (with one exception) were all Hysterical affections, originating in the same cause; that they were of a nature similar to the five cases that were previously discussed; and that they would have been arrested and dispersed by an adoption of similar measures.

In all these cases, as may be seen in the reports of them, catamenial suppression preceded the other manifestations; and dissection, in one case, demonstrated the existence of intense excitement of all the uterine organs. Yet it is a little remarkable, that not one of the eminent men into whose hands these cases fell, has even suggested the probability of this suppression being instrumental to the development of the ensuing symptoms; neither are we led to conjecture, that the spinal marrow and its membranes were supposed to be implicated, in more than one of them, or that these were examined, in the only way possible, by pressure, or the application of heat. Considering the fearfully long duration of some of them, this is strange and surprising; for, certainly, if there be any one structure of the body in which, *à priori*, we should expect to discover the source of these varied affections, the spinal marrow is that structure; and here we should commence the search, with the greatest probability of success. But, as before remarked, in the majority of instances, no pain is felt in this part by the patient; nor is there any uneasiness, until pressure or heat is applied; and then it is that complaint is invariably made in the way I have pointed out; and to this rule I cannot remember an exception.

CHAPTER VIII.

HYSTERIA OF THE THIRD DEGREE.

In the preceding divisions of this essay, I have confined the reader's attention to those classes of Hysterical disorders which are sometimes difficult to identify, owing to their great variety, and to their simulation of other complaints; but yet, under a well regulated management, are not, generally, of very tedious duration.

I am now coming to the consideration of cases of a more aggravated and, sometimes, of an almost hopeless description. It must, however, be still understood, that between these and the cases before related there is no substantial distinction, except as refers to their different duration. They are made up of the same materials, occur under the same peculiar circumstances, and are to be cured, when curable at all, by much the same kind of measures. A deranged state of the uterine functions, *quoad* the catamenia, is the forerunner and the *sine quâ non* of both; but in the former kind, generally, the disorder is ushered suddenly in by some violent and alarming symptom, with very little, if any, premonitory illness; whilst the cases with which we have now to deal usually steal on by slow degrees, for many months, without any *violent eruption,* until the patient either sinks into a state of deplorable debility, or some extraordinary symptoms supervene, similar to those before described.

It must not then be supposed, that because violence and convulsive symptoms are absent, therefore the case cannot be purely Hysterical. These are, unfortunately, the worst kind of Hysterical disorders; because, being masked, as it were, they are so much the more liable to be misunderstood. It does not follow, that because convulsion and contractions frequently accompany Hysteria, it cannot occur without them: these do not compose its essentials. Its essentials are, firstly, a deranged menstruation; secondly, spinal irritation; and, in consequence of this latter associating the whole corporeal system in disorder with itself, by means of the Par Vagum and Great Sympathetic nerves, convulsions and spasms, of every variety, are produced; but these, although consequences, are not necessary consequences of such original disturbance. The usual marks of Hysteria are frequently present without any variable or striking phenomena; and if the practitioner knows what these are, he will generally be able to distinguish them from actual disease, and will not then be dealing his blows at random, in the dark, and mistaking a phantom for a substantial foe. But, at present, we see eminent physicians falling into this fatal snare; treating Hysterical aches and pains as active diseases, and oftentimes not discovering their error, *until it is* too late to repair it.

Yet even these cases, crippling as they are to the health and comfort of young women, are still, perhaps, not dangerous to life, if life that existence may be called, which is robbed of all enjoyment, and of all expectation of returning health: for, if misunderstood, and treated rashly or ignorantly, they will be often fatal to the happiness of the patient, plunging her into an age of suffering and misery; to say nothing of that "hope deferred, which maketh the heart sick." Under the best management, these cases which have been neglected in their early stages are sometimes prolonged to such a period, that they become almost as sickening to the practitioner as to the patient herself. I know scarcely anything more mortifying to our pathology and treatment of disease, than the obstinate resistance made by these disorders to the means directed against them; and yet, unless a case has been of very long standing, or very disgracefully tampered with, a well regulated treatment will rarely fail to restore the patient, ultimately, to a state of moderate health and vigour.

As there is no regular set of symptoms that admit, as in common diseases, of being set forth as universally present to mark its nature, I must content myself with a general description of this form of Hysteria, leaving the body of the picture to be filled up by a report of cases. As before stated, in the most tedious form of Hysteria, *menstruation* is always more or less faulty at the *onset; and as the* case advances, this becomes suppressed altogether, or is performed very sparingly, perhaps only once in many months, and then with great pain. Where this function is quite suspended, there is, generally, neither any periodical pain, nor any sensation, to show that nature had not forgotten this customary duty. Shortly afterwards, the patient becomes weak and desponding, loses her appetite, and the bloom from her cheeks. She has still nothing particular to complain of, and, generally, keeps up her flesh, although it has every appearance of relaxation. If a medical man sees her now, he will find her with a moist and tremulous tongue; being foul at the root, and having the papillæ, at that part, larger than natural, and like little tubercles; with a tainted breath; depraved taste; little or no appetite; with a weak, languid pulse; with a sickly, yellowish complexion; black or clay-coloured alvine secretions, and the urine highly coloured and scanty. In a little time, she will have pain under the left breast, which is increased by deep inspiration, and by reclining upon that side,—sometimes pain also in the right side, palpitations, flutterings, sinkings; and, together with these, there will be pain upon pressure in one or more parts of the spine: first of all, in three or four of the dorsal vertebræ; generally, also, in the lumbar; and, if the case be very lasting, it sometimes extends up to the very summit of the cervical portion. In such cases, the head-aches are intolerable; being in some instances constant, in others interrupted, but always violent. The mischief may not end here.

In process of time the slightest light becomes intolerable; so much so, that the patient may remain for weeks together with her face buried in the pillow to avoid the least exposure of the eyes.

In the midst of all this, she is not much reduced in flesh, and, for a considerable time, it is not sensibly diminished. As the disease advances, a number of anomalous pains of a neuralgic character become associated with the other symptoms. Thus, if pressure be made upon the supra or infra-orbital nerves, upon the inferior maxillary, &c., as they issue from their foramina, considerable pain is produced; but these spots are seldom complained of, in the absence of such pressure. It is not, however, the facial nerves that are alone implicated; for almost every nerve in the body becomes, at the same time, endued with a similar increase of sensibility. This sort of neuralgic affection is seldom observed until the case is far advanced, and has become equally inveterate and puzzling.

The early stage of such a condition as this will prevail for eighteen months, before any particular notice is taken of it by the patient, or her friends: she gets gradually worse, until some sudden spasmodic affection, or other unaccountable symptom, commands attention; and then medical advice is obtained. At other times, where more solicitude is felt, advice is obtained at an earlier period; and the patient is called a dyspeptic, or a *hypochondriac*, or a nervous lady; and, if judiciously treated, will gradually recover her health.

The following is an example of very protracted Hysteria, which was aggravated by the manner in which it was maltreated.

Case 15.

Miss —— became a patient of mine after an illness of ten years' standing; in the course of which she had been, at different times, under the management of twelve different practitioners. Some of these were of high reputation: but those of a high, and those of a less elevated rank, were equally unsuccessful in their attempts to restore her to health, or even to give her more than transient relief. This was, of course, very discouraging information. She had menstruated at the age of fifteen, and soon afterwards her illness took place; commencing with a total suppression of the catamenia, which was referred, at the time, to cold. When I first saw her, she had just returned from a watering-place, was so weak that it was with difficulty she could walk across the room, and was obliged to be carried to and from her apartment. Her complexion was sallow, her lips bloodless, pulse small and quick, tongue loaded with a thick, yellowish-brown, moist secretion, bowels torpid, the water uniformly clear and natural. There was a fixed and lancinating pain in a hollow between the cartilages of the fifth and sixth ribs of *the left* side; pain under the margin of the ribs of the right side, considerable difficulty of breathing, and frequent violent palpitations. The headaches were almost incessant, and often nearly distracting by their violence. There was pain upon pressure throughout the cervical and dorsal vertebræ; and pressure between the shoulders aggravated the dyspnœa. She was sometimes seized with an uncontrollable vomiting, which lasted seven or eight days together; at which times, not a spoonful of cold water would remain upon her stomach: these attacks were ultimately tranquillized by opiate suppositaries, leaving her strength completely prostrate. She scarcely ever closed her eyes to sleep, although her sufferings were so great, that she was lying in a recumbent posture, at times, for days and nights together, with her eyes shut in silent agony. She appeared literally not to eat anything. She had not menstruated since the beginning of her illness, when she was near sixteen years of age. Upon inquiring whether any examination of the spinal column had been made by the different gentlemen who had attended her, I was told, that about four years before, a physician had traced the spine with his fingers, and she complained that the pressure was disagreeable at several points; but the surgeon who accompanied him observed, that this tenderness "arose from the position in which she was lying," and no further notice was taken of it. After hearing the indifferent success which had *resulted from* the labours of my brethren in this *young lady's* behalf, and after trying my own ingenuity in getting rid of the pain in the left side, of which she chiefly complained, (and which was so incessant and wearying, that she enjoyed no interval of ease or of rest,) with the same bad success, I began to consider that this case was altogether Hysterical, and that the pain in the side proceeded from the spinal irritation. It was then that I instituted an examination which verified this opinion, by discovering that nearly the whole extent of the vertebral column was more tender than it would be in a state of health. Her health and strength were now so much reduced, that I was determined to wait patiently for nature to recover herself a little, before anything else was done for her. She continued to fluctuate from better to worse every few days; was extremely dejected, and every slight vexation or surprise threw her into a fit of "Hysterics;" which, however, sometimes took place unprovoked by any mental emotion. At length, a tartar emetic plaster was applied in the course of the vertebræ, which occasioned great distress; and the sickness, unfortunately, returned about this time with more than usual violence, which she and her friends ascribed to the plaster, whether justly or not it is hard to say. Be that as it may, no persuasions could ever afterwards induce her to submit to its re-application; and she thought she had good reason for her contumacy, since, as she said, the first plaster had given her excessive pain, had not relieved her side, but had added the sickness to it. *It was* consequently abandoned, very reluctantly by me, as I had great confidence in its virtues. Mild aperients were taken to regulate the bowels, and she gradually regained a little strength. Cold evaporating lotions were applied to the head, and the other pains were suffered to take their chance for a short time. As she improved, I was induced to try the carbonate of iron, as the pain between the fifth and sixth ribs was stationary, and was evidently neuralgic. It was exhibited with all possible caution, but again produced the much dreaded sickness, and was discontinued. She afterwards went to Cheltenham, where I occasionally saw her, in consultation with a celebrated physician of that place. A small eschar was made over the seat of pain, by the lapis infernalis, and a discharge promoted by peas; but to no purpose. After a short interval, the carbonate of iron was again taken, and it now did not appear to offend the stomach. The quantity taken at each dose was increased, by slow degrees, from a scruple to half an ounce, three times a day; so that, at last, she may be said to have lived upon iron. Under this plan she rallied very remarkably, and we were in hopes of seeing her perfectly recover. Her side was much better, the bowels acting favourably; the head-aches were now trifling, and the spinal tenderness scarcely perceptible. The catamenia appeared once very sparingly, but never returned. She was able to walk and ride out, and was better than she had been for years. In this state, she went to the neighbourhood of Bath; and, under the direction of an eminent surgeon, was bled once a fortnight. When it was first proposed, she wrote to me upon the subject, and was strongly advised not to submit to so life-destroying a treatment. However, the surgeon told her that he had once effected a cure, by this practice, *in a similar case*; and it accordingly was put in force. For twenty-four successive fortnights, this was continued; at the end of that time, she returned to my care. She had not been bled for many weeks, as, upon the last occasion that this operation was performed, a long and deep syncope ensued, from which she was with difficulty recovered. She had now an irregular pulse, violent palpitations, œdematous legs, even to the knees, cold extremities, shortness of breath, and a countenance indicative of exhaustion and distress. The left breast was very much wasted, as were also some of the muscles on the side of the chest; producing a degree of deformity that was evident through her clothes. I entreated her to subject herself to no more such ruinous experiments; but to take wholesome food; to take as much exercise as her strength would bear, short of fatigue; to take no medicine but a tonic-aperient pill; and to use the shower-bath twice, and the warm hip-bath three times, a week. She then proceeded to Leamington, where she has followed these directions. Her health improves, but the wasting and numbness of the left breast and side are making gradual progress. There appears little hope of her complete recovery, although she has already endured little short of a quarter of an ordinary life of diversified suffering.

It will be confessed, that this was an instance of prolonged and established disease, resulting from original error, and a continued series of malpractice. From the onset of the patient's illness, the pain in her side, and dyspnœa, had been the ostensible points of complaint; and throughout the early years of their continuance depletory measures were adopted by every practitioner into whose hands she fell. Her natural power was thus paralysed, and disabled from exerting itself in the right direction, by restoring the catamenia; the suppression of which was the cause of her first deviation from health, and the restoration of which should have been made a first principle in the treatment. Instead of this, the pain in the side was regarded as the main symptom, and was supposed to indicate pleuritic or some other visceral inflammation; and measures for its extinction were pursued with more boldness than prudence or judgment. This pain, however, was merely a small part of a most extensive disorder, totally unconnected with any derangement, structural or functional, of the contents of the chest, utterly uncontrollable by the lancet, and only to be relieved by improving the general health, and removing the spinal irritation, with which it has some inexplicable connexion.

If it be said, that this was not a case of Hysteria, I must ask, by what other name it can be called. The whole case rested upon the catamenial suspension. Then followed the pain in the side, the dyspnœa, the palpitations, the vertebral tenderness, and, in addition to these, the Hysterical paroxysms, which were continually taking place upon slight occasions, and sometimes without any *obvious* exciting cause. But, call it what you will, it is certain (or so probable as to be almost certain) that, had a mild and judicious course been followed in the first place, instead of a lowering one, the patient would have soon been liberated from a complaint that will now be her companion for the remainder of an unhappy life.

Were a case such as this of solitary, or even of rare, occurrence, I should not have devoted so many pages to its narration; nor have taken what some may consider the invidious pains of pointing out the mistaken views that were entertained of it. But the fact is far otherwise. Such cases and corresponding errors are "as plenty as blackberries." Daily are young people afflicted with this very pain under the left breast, bled, blistered, leeched, cupped, and passed through a long course of depleting and enervating medicines, when there is no earthly necessity for it, and when, instead of benefitting them, the pain is unmitigated, and the debility increased a hundredfold. Finding this system fail of its intended effect, the patient is frequently supposed to be falling into consumption, or dying of diseased heart, or some other atrocious malady; and thus is the happiness of many a family compromised, and a painful anxiety substituted in its stead.

The more enlightened and practised members of the profession well know that the evils of which I have spoken are not imaginary, and that it is not unnecessary to warn young practitioners against the commission of such flagrant mistakes; for not one case out of a hundred, in which this pain in the side is a prominent grievance, and of some standing, attended by obstructed or otherwise depraved menstruation, will give way to the reducing system, which is so frequently and so fatally enforced, and of which the case just related is deplorably illustrative. In this instance, the nerves proceeding from the dorsal vertebræ for the supply of the muscles and coverings of the left breast and side, ultimately lost much of their influence, and these parts became shrunk and paralysed. There appears little hope that they will ever be restored; as it is probable, that the cause of the loss of substance and of sensibility consists in structural lesion of a portion of the left side of the spinal marrow itself, or of the nerves at their emergence, which neither time nor art can repair.

I now proceed to the description of a case, the character of which, whatever may be thought of the former, is as unquestionable as it was intractable.

Case 16.

Charlotte L. was a domestic in a gentleman's family. *During* her service the catamenia appeared for the first time, at the age of sixteen, but did not visit her again. Some months afterwards, she complained of head-aches and shortness of breath, which continued some time, but no notice was taken of them. These were soon followed by pain and weakness in the legs, together with aching of the arms and tingling in the hands. No medical assistance was sought for, and she returned to her parents. Here again she was thought weak and nervous, and nothing was done for her until pain under the left breast, palpitations, twitching of the hands and of the feet, were added to the other symptoms. A practitioner of the neighbourhood now attended her, and, although I did not know the whole of his treatment, she had been twice largely bled, and it was sufficiently evident, when I first saw her, that she had been profusely salivated; the gums being spongy and turgid, fauces ulcerated, breath mercurial, and streams of saliva issuing from her mouth. I first saw her about twelve months after the beginning of her illness. The following is an imperfect description of her condition at that period. She was lying in a most helpless state, without the least power of moving herself voluntarily a single inch from the place in which she was laid; and when raised up in bed, her body fell about, by its gravity, like a dead thing. She could answer questions very inarticulately, in the lowest whisper. Her intellects were unimpaired, though she complained violently of her head, and had not *opened* her eyes for more than four months. This is a singular fact, that the impatience of light was so urgent, that she had not seen daylight for more than four months. There was an incessant quivering of the lids, but they were never so far separated as to allow any portion of the eye to be seen. When the lid was raised, to examine the pupil, nothing was visible but the white of the eye; its whole front being imbedded in the arch of the orbit. The hearing was natural. Her arms were spasmodically contracted, her hands clenched, binding down the thumbs; the legs similarly affected. The dyspnœa and pain in the side were unabated. Pressure upon the spine, in any part of the dorsal portion, occasioned her much pain. She had been able to swallow no nourishment for two months, but a little gruel and water daily; yet had she had not shrunk in flesh to any great degree, although her strength was quite prostrate, her pulse small and quick, urine scanty and high-coloured. Alvine secretions dark, and only evacuated once in five or six days. She was now upwards of seventeen years old, and the catamenia had not re-appeared.

After hearing the history of the case, no hesitation was necessary as to its nature or treatment. The head was immediately shaved. The tartar emetic ointment was applied all over the scalp, and down the whole extent of the spinal column. A profuse crop of pustules followed. Aloetics, with salts and senna, were then given her in considerable quantity, as the bowels were exceedingly inactive. As soon as the eruption was developed, she could open her eyes for a few moments at a time, and her hands became relaxed: in three weeks she could bear the light tolerably well, and no contraction of the hands or of any other part remained. She took food, and suffered very little pain, save that arising from the pustulation, which, however, was considerable. As she improved, my visits were discontinued. She went on well for some time, was able to walk about the house, but did not recover her strength. She continued to lose flesh, although her appetite was good, and she took much more nourishment than before. She persevered in taking aloetics and iron, in hopes of restoring the menses, but these did not appear; and after continuing for six months in about the same state, apparently without any absolute disorder, she fell back into a worse state than that from which she had been recovering. She was now a most deplorable object, a perfect skeleton, with the exception of her cheeks and breasts; the former having a healthy bloom, and the latter being tolerably full and firm. It is a singular circumstance, that these, throughout her illness, did not lose altogether their usual plump appearance. Her pulse was languid, and never more than sixty; she sighed frequently and deeply. Her tongue was clean and tremulous, and from the fauces was a continual trickling of fluid; which had some tenacity, and was said to be sometimes the colour of blood. The admission of light was again very painful, but she could open her eyes a little, and the pupils were always dilated. Her skin was dry and husky, but cool. There was a sense of constriction, and of pain across the precordial region. Her legs and arms were contracted nearly in the same manner as before; in addition to which, the arms were frequently affected with a kind of rotatory motion, which was very violent whenever she happened to be disturbed by questions or alterations of posture; and mostly terminated in general spasm, by which the whole body was drawn into a heap, causing considerable suffering at the time, and subsequent exhaustion.

A blister was placed upon the spine, but not the least relief was derived from it; and now even a few words addressed to her produced intense spasms of all the flexor muscles, in addition to those of the limbs. Her head was drawn down, so that the face was hidden in her bosom; and, during this time, the *Sterno-cleido-mastoid* was curiously affected, acting spasmodically, and thus occasioning a constant nodding of the head, which lasted for more than a quarter of an hour at a time, and gradually went off as the muscles became tired. Emaciated as she was, I determined, for the third time, to pustulate the whole occiput and spine with the tartar emetic; as this appeared, at last, to be the only measure that gave her a prospect of relief. After a few applications, this was effected, and, immediately afterwards, the spasms and involuntary actions ceased. They never again returned. She, by degrees, became more sensible, could bear more light, answer questions collectedly, and all her limbs, which had been spell-bound for so many weeks, were released, and might be moved at will in any direction. She took some little nourishment, for which she still had a great aversion; and many months elapsed, before she regained even a moderate portion of health or strength.

Case 17.

This was a different kind of case from any of the foregoing. It was *Hysteric Cough.* The subject was a young lady of seventeen. She had been ill for more than twelve months, and had been attended, before I saw her, by a gentleman who considered it symptomatic of pulmonary disease. During the whole of this time, the periodical secretion, which had been previously healthy, was of a very depraved character, being as dingy as if it had been commingled with soot; and its evacuation was attended with so much agony, that she was compelled to keep her bed at each visitation, although its regular periods were preserved. The cough was of a peculiar kind; resembling none of those met with in diseases of the pulmonary or bronchial structures, or in those more urgent of the larynx. It was a short convulsive cough, which seemed to arise from a spasmodic action of the diaphragm; and (if I attempt its description in words) was more like a half-stifled bark, than any other sound. It did not consist of violent, interrupted fits, as if for the expulsion of some *irritating* matter; but was a short, quick, insulated bark, always made with the mouth shut, which shook her whole frame; was exasperated by any surprise, by the least change of temperature, or by any allusion that was made to it in her presence. This is the usual kind of cough that prevails in Hysteria, which it is of great importance to know. In addition to the cough, were pain in the left side, soreness over the whole chest, from almost incessant action; rapidity and shortness of breath; palpitations; pain across the loins and in the legs; quick pulse; torpid bowels: but the tongue was clean, and she slept well; the cough being less urgent at night, but continuing at intervals. The patient had lost little flesh, but much of her strength; indeed, she could with difficulty walk fifty yards. Upon examination of the back, she complained of tenderness in the dorsal vertebræ, and the same when heat was applied; which confirmed my first opinion of the nature of the case. She had been several times bled, blistered, leeched, and otherwise treated in accordance with the view entertained by her former attendant; all which had served only to puzzle him, and reduce the patient, without obtaining the least advantage over the disorder. The tartar emetic was now employed in the usual way, upon the spinal column, to some extent: and some active cathartics, as calomel and aloes, were prescribed for her. Under this regulation, she got rapidly better. When the catamenial period approached, a mixture, with laudanum, was taken, which alleviated the usual pain, but did not remove it, until the same had been pursued for several returns. As soon as the eruption declared itself, the cough was less violent and less frequent; and, after a second application, with the combined aid of aloetics and exercise, it disappeared, and she became, in a little time, perfectly well; and has continued so up to the present period.

Another form, in which Hysteria sometimes presents itself, may be seen in the following particulars.

Case 18.

Miss A. G., aged nineteen years, having been in a weak state of health some months, was suddenly attacked with giddiness and violent pain in the forehead one evening, at a place of public diversion. She returned home in a fainting, half-insensible state. She was bled and physicked, but the vertigo and pain continued, in spite of every thing that was done to remove them. She had lingered on in this way nearly twelve months, when I first attended her. She then complained of giddiness of a peculiar kind; which she described as a violent rocking motion, which made her feel as if she could not possibly keep her balance, whenever she rose upon her feet. This was attended by darting pains through the head, in addition to a constant dull aching and stupor, with various unpleasant sensations. When the pain was violent, the conjunctive membrane of the eye became injected and watery; the nerves, above and below the orbit, were also very tender, when pressed upon at their emergence from the bone. These were accompanied by pain below the left breast, frequent and strong palpitations, globus Hystericus; and pain in the throat, loaded tongue, and slow bowels. She had a very quick, but regular and expanded pulse, and a healthy and natural expression of countenance. The proper periods of menstruation were not disturbed, but the secretion was scanty, and of very depraved quality; its appearance having been, ever since the commencement of her illness, preceded and attended by severe distress. The spinal column was tender throughout the dorsal divisions, but the most painful were the third, fourth, fifth, and sixth dorsal, and the three uppermost cervical vertebræ; which could not bear any pressure, or the approach of a hot sponge, without pain of a very sensible kind. These circumstances amply convinced me, that the case was purely Hysterical; and, after a satisfactory investigation, I pronounced an opinion of its favourable and speedy issue. In part of this prognostic, I was, however, disappointed, as it turned out a very tedious and troublesome affair. The tartar emetic, in this case, did not answer my expectations. The first application relieved the head, certainly, and diminished the lateral pain and palpitation; but these all returned soon after the eruption died away. Yet such was my confidence in its efficacy, that it was again and again resorted to; but unfortunately the symptoms reappeared, although other means were taken, and *successfully, to* restore the internal organs to a *healthy state,*—aloetics, steel, warm bath, shower bath, &c. The carbonate of iron was taken to a great extent, and at first seemed of much service, but it did not long sanction this opinion. During the whole of this time, the spine continued more or less tender, at the same points. Two physicians were called in while she was under my care. The one acknowledged himself utterly ignorant of the case, and the other assured her that "when her heart got well, her head would get well." They both prescribed for her, with such success as might have been anticipated, from the satisfactory view each had taken of the subject upon which his advice was required. Instead of growing better, she retrograded under the weakening plan that was now followed. At length, when my patience was nearly exhausted, and her own hopes were becoming desperate, I persuaded her to abandon all kinds of medicine; to blister the spine extensively, and repeatedly; to lead a very regular life; to take carriage exercise daily, and leave the rest to nature. The motion of the vehicle produced, at first, faintness, and dreadful sensations in the head; but after the operation of the first blister, she could bear it better; and, by the time the third had done its work, her complaints had vanished, and did not revisit her afterwards.

Here, then, was an instance, and almost the only instance that occurred to me, in which blisters succeeded after the ointment had failed.

This young lady, from first to last, was ill about three years: in the course of this time a variety of *opposite* measures were suggested for her relief;

but little or no advantage resulted from them. Venesection, leeches to the head, to the spine, to the side, pustulation, evaporating lotions to the head, purgatives, tonics, shower and warm baths, were all tried, and all found wanting. Such discrepant remedies were not, however, productive of signal injury to her, as she had the happiness to possess much natural robustness; neither was she much weaker at the latter part than at the beginning of her illness; as was evinced by the rapid manner in which she recovered after the giddiness, pains, and palpitations ceased.

CHAPTER IX.

This list of cases might be extended to a much greater length, as there remain many forms of disorder the character of which is assumed by Hysteria, all varying in some particulars, that have not been here detailed: such detail, indeed, would be impossible, there being scarcely a single disease or disorder that Hysteria may not resemble, from the simplest to the most formidable of human maladies. Yet, under proper management, they are unattended with danger; and, even under a misguided treatment, will generally give way to time, and the strong inclination of dame Nature to return into her ordinary course; although she certainly, sometimes, deviates from it upon very slight provocation.

It is not uncommon, for example, for Hysteria to put on all the characters of pregnancy; the catamenia being suppressed,—the breasts becoming tumid and painful,—the abdomen enlarging, together with sickness and pain in the back: and it sometimes requires the keenest discrimination to be satisfied of the non-existence of pregnancy. It will generally be found in such cases, that the catamenia had been long irregular before suppression took place; that the abdominal enlargement is not uniform, but varying from day to day; and there will be other Hysterical symptoms present: but, in some instances, even where the reputation is perfectly spotless, nothing but the progress of time, or examination *per vaginam,* will reduce the matter to certainty.

A short time back, a fine young woman, suffering under the like symptoms, was brought from the country for my advice, her character having sustained great disparagement in the estimation of all her neighbours and friends, in consequence of her presenting all the outward signs of pregnancy. Having ascertained the nature of the case, I ordered her a course of aloetics, sending her back to her own neighbourhood during her cure, in order that those who had accused her might be convinced, by her gradual recovery and diminution in bulk, of the injustice of the charge against her.

The case of the late unfortunate Lady Flora Hastings, which some years ago excited so much sympathy and surprise, and which was most discreditable to the acumen of Sir James Clark, was, no doubt, one of this description.

In another case of the kind, a young girl of nineteen was persuaded by some old women that she was pregnant; which, from a consciousness of some irregularity of conduct, she was prepared to believe. The time came when she was supposed to be taken in labour, and a midwife attended. After three days' anxious waiting, and feeling great alarm, her friends sent for me; when, to the amazement of midwife and patient, I declared her *not to be pregnant.*

In these cases, a course of powerful aloetics will

restore the abdomen to its natural proportions. In what its engorgement consists, it is difficult to determine: it is not a mere accumulation in the colon, yet that it is substantial is equally certain. Probably the spleen, as well as the ovaries, are congested; and there may be, also, an increase of fatty deposit in the omentum and mesentery.

Again, dropsy is not a very rare appearance in Hysterical females. I knew a young woman, in whose abdomen there was a distinct, but, as it turned out, deceptive feeling of fluctuation; leading me to suspect the existence of Ovarian cysts. Her general health was very little disturbed, but menstruation had been suspended for six months, and she had strong hysterical paroxysms. A course of purgative medicines proved the nature of the case, and completely cured the patient.

A curious case of this kind has been lately recorded, but in what publication it appeared I now forget. Tumefaction of the abdomen, with evident fluctuation, having existed for some time, disappeared upon the eruption of the menses. Soon afterwards, the swelling and sense of fluctuation became again distinct, increasing rapidly for a month, till the catamenia came; they then subsided. This was repeated time after time, the dropsical symptoms always disappearing after the performance of menstruation, till at last the patient got well.

Notwithstanding the manifest signs of fluctuation that appeared to be present, I cannot but entertain some doubt of the real existence of hydropic effusion in the abdominal cavity; although, certainly, swelling to that extent could not have taken place without some sufficient mechanical cause. The following anecdote which Sir Astley Cooper used to relate, and which I repeat from memory, will prove that it is possible for eminent surgeons to form erroneous opinions, and to make fatal mistakes, in regard to abdominal fluctuation.

"A woman was brought into the operating theatre, in a Parisian hospital, to be tapped for Dropsy. The surgeon introduced his trocar; but upon withdrawing the stilet, no fluid escaped. Supposing that he had not made the puncture low enough to open the sac, he plunged in his instrument at an inferior part. Here again he was disappointed, as no water could by any means be evacuated, although it was persuaded by a third immersion of the trocar. He, at last, became satisfied that there was no dropsy; and, nothing daunted, turned round and addressed his class, with much gravity, in nearly the following words: —'Gentlemen, this is an operation which, perhaps, *many* of you have never seen before; and it is, moreover, an operation which, in all probability, *none* of you will ever see again. This is called *Dry-tapping!*'—The patient was removed, and what happened afterwards may be easily guessed."

Whilst speaking of the simulation by Hysteria of abdominal diseases, it may be stated, that one of the common complaints in Hysterical habits is a violent and constant intonation in the abdomen, called "*Clangor Intestinorum.*" This is excited by any mental emotion, and is so loud and continuous as to compel the patient to quit the room, or to shun society altogether. It arises from irregular and persistent peristaltic action, connected with the presence of flatus; and is generally to be corrected by a course of valerian and hydrochloric acid. At other times, there are attacks of Borborygma, as they are called; these consist in repeated and almost incessant expulsions of wind from the stomach. They are loud enough to be heard over a whole house of moderate size, and arise from a very rapid and enormous generation of gas in the stomach, which is often so sudden as to threaten the patient with suffocation, though, of course, of that there is no serious danger.

There is another kind of Hysteria, in which all the abdominal muscles are thrown into violent convulsive action, undulating up and down in a most tumultuous manner; as if the whole contents of the abdomen were being flung up to the throat and back again with great force and rapidity, and almost suffocating the patient. These symptoms are as obstinate as any other form of the disorder, unless properly understood. They are accompanied by tenderness of the spine, and pain in the side, and such phenomena as belong to other forms of the disorder. The most tremendous and distressing case of this kind that I ever witnessed, was plied with numerous remedies of one sort or another, but yielded to nothing, till the antimonial ointment was used, and the exhibitions were then at an end.

A species of Hysteria sometimes arises, though fortunately it is not of frequent occurrence, in which all the nerves of sensation become so blunted, that there is an entire loss of feeling over the whole surface of the body. Combined with this state of things, there may be a good deal of mental perverseness. This kind of paralysis occasionally extends to the bladder, making a resort to the catheter appear necessary. Now there is no doubt that in these remarkable cases it is safe to trust to nature, without the use of the catheter, for an almost indefinite period. If the surgeon will only have patience and courage to delay the use of the instrument, he will generally be rewarded by seeing his patient relieved by natural means; and when so relieved, the difficulty will not often recur: but *once* resort to the instrument, and it is impossible to foretell how long it may be before it can be dispensed with. Early in life, finding an immensely distended bladder, and apprehensive of rupture, or something almost equally appalling, I have relieved the patient by the catheter; but experience has convinced me that, however great the distress may be arising from the retention of urine, it is an error to afford relief by the catheter until every other resource shall have been tried, and failed. Large sinapisms to the lumbar portion of the spine, and dashing cold water upon the bowels and hips, with powerful emetics, will be almost sure to succeed, if persevered in; but should everything fail, the catheter must be used. It cannot be too strongly urged, that instrumental relief may in these cases be prudently delayed far beyond the time that in ordinary circumstances it would be safe to leave the patient; but relief by the instrument is so easy, while the consequences of rupture are so fearful, that the first course is the one usually preferred, especially as it will generally be encouraged, if not enforced, by the patient and her friends, as offering immediate relief from very severe distress. Still a medical man should never forget, in his anxiety to give temporary relief, that his first duty is to aim at the permanent cure of his patient.

Sometimes this paralytic affection takes another form, consequent upon which the hands and feet become gradually twisted into the most shapeless postures, the patient becoming a piece of helpless lumber. Yet even such a case, if it be rightly understood, is by no means desperate or hopeless. Indeed, unreasonable as it may seem, it is possible that a restoration of the limbs to their natural state may be established more easily at a remote period than at an earlier stage of the illness. The explanation is this: the abnormal shape arises from Hysterical paralysis, which may attack only the nerves of one side of the legs, arms, hands, and fingers; (common paralysis generally striking one *whole* limb, or one side of the body;) the effect of which is a contortion of the hands, fingers, or other parts, consequent upon increased contraction of the unaffected muscles, during the suspension of power on the paralysed side, thus producing much deformity. The paralysis sooner or later goes off, but the deformity is suffered to remain, under the mistaken belief in its permanence. This is a great error; for this paralysis *never* is permanent, nor is it a work of difficulty by means of proper appliances to re-establish the balance of power, and to restore the limbs to their natural form and usefulness.

Some years ago, a case fell under my care, in which the deformity had existed from the age of 17 to 30, and it was surprising to see the easy and ready way in which the distorted limbs yielded to treatment, and resumed their former state.

It should never be forgotten in these cases, as well as in many others, that if you can succeed in removing preventive causes, Nature is always most desirous to return from any devious step she may have taken, back into her own proper channel.

Simulated or spurious disease of the hip-joint is not an uncommon Hysterical affection; but although the fact that Hysteria will occasionally take this form is generally known, yet when it does occur, almost every surgeon suffers himself to be duped and deceived by it. Attention to the rules laid down in the foregoing pages is sufficient to mark the distinction between the true disease, and that which is a mere chimera; and a man of sound common sense, and a fair share of *observing power*, need never be imposed upon.

It is needless to multiply examples of these cases. Sufficient has been written to sustain the importance of the subject, and to lead young practitioners to a more correct knowledge, and to a juster appreciation of the nature of Hysterical affections, than are generally acquired until after years of bad practice, bad success, and harassing anxieties.

The treatment is, generally, very simple and successful; and what the practitioner fails to perform, nature will often do for him; so that, having ascertained its identity, if he will only abstain from doing too much, he may rest tolerably well assured of its fortunate result. The diagnosis of Hysteria thus becomes of still greater importance than its treatment; as the principal difficulty consists in penetrating the disguises it assumes, and in recognising its real features under them. Ignorant of this qualification, a man will run great risk of injuring his patient by a blind practice, and of damaging his own reputation by a blind and falsified prophecy.

Perhaps the following case of supposed disease of the Hip-joint may set forth, more clearly than any arguments, the mischiefs resulting to patient and practitioner from such mistakes as those before spoken of. Some time ago I went to see an old friend of my youth, a lady whom I had not seen for many months. She told me that one of her daughters, a girl of nineteen, was in a most dreadful state; that she had disease of the hip-joint; and that the doctors had prepared her mind for the worst. She added, that the girl's sufferings were so terrible, that she not only looked forward to her death, but anxiously desired its approach. I remembered that, about twelve months before, she was said to have a disease of the spine, and was laid upon her back for some time; but, for the last three months, the pain had been confined to her hip, and the whole length of her leg; for which she had been leeched, blistered, cupped, and had suffered the formation of caustic issues; but all in vain. The disease made progress, and, when I called, the medical men were daily expecting to see a shortening of the limb take place. Her mother, in describing the case, said, that she had, first of all, complained of stiffness in the right knee, and difficulty of raising it; so that in walking only from chair to chair, she was obliged to join her hands under the ham, and so help herself along. By and by this grew worse, till her limb was contracted; the thigh being drawn up in front, and the leg behind, as if she were slightly trussed. She then kept her bed. Violent pain now came on in her hip, and the pain and spasm, at last, wandered into the other leg also. This was supposed to arise from sympathy. Her convulsions were dreadful, and she screamed out frequently with great violence; particularly when an attempt was made to move her. She was reduced to a skeleton, and there was sloughing over the hip-bone from a bed-sore; motion being so extremely painful, that for six weeks her bed had not been made, neither had her position been in the least changed. This story struck me as being a strange history of disease of the hip-joint, and led me to make a further inquiry. The following circumstances then transpired. About twelve months ago, she was very Hysterical, and had dreadful pains in her back, which were supposed to arise from a disease of the spine. The catamenia were then very irregular, and attended with much pain. This had continued to the present time. She had, all along, complained of pain under the left breast, and sometimes in the right side, which felt as if a knife were piercing her. She had been subject to palpitations, which were now very distressing. She had tremendous headaches, and was sometimes, at night, delirious. She had intolerance of light, and the room was darkened accordingly; she had globus and dyspnœa; Hysterical feelings without number, and a most capricious state of mind. Notwithstanding all this, the doctors could see nothing but disease of the hip-joint; yet there was no decisive or obvious mark of disease,—no swelling or puffing about the hip,—no increase of pain upon pressure,—and, as well as could be ascertained by their measurement, in the position in which she was lying, there was no difference in the length of the limbs. To make the case more apparent, there was now a similar contraction of the other thigh, and a similar pain in the other limb. She now also complained of pain in her spine, which, she said, was like the flesh being torn away from the bone. This catalogue of circumstances combined together, thoroughly satisfied me that this was an Hysterical case, which had been most unfortunately mistaken and mistreated. She had now taken a rooted dislike to her medical attendants; declared (and with good show of reason) that no doctors could do her any good, and that all she wanted was to be suffered to die in peace. I represented to her mother what was the source and nature of the illness, and ventured to express great confidence in her recovery, provided she were, even now, to be invigorated by a nourishing diet, and proper treatment were sedulously employed. This advice was attended to, and with success; for, after a long and painful struggle, her better stars prevailed, and she was restored to health.

A memorable case, very similar in many of its features, occurred at Brompton in the year 1847, in which Brodie, Liston, and other metropolitan stars, were consulted, besides the local surgeons. They all expressed most unfavourable opinions of the case, as resulting from organic disease; and Mr. Liston, in particular, pronounced for a carious state of the vertebral bones, which was to end in death. Indeed, for months, the family believed the young lady to be in a dying state. Her sufferings were absolutely frightful, and prolonged almost beyond the verge of belief. Yet, in spite of these, and of the judgment of so many eminent men, there was in this case neither real disease nor danger, and death was very distant indeed; for she has now been married several years, with spine and limbs in perfect shape and form, and is in full possession of all her faculties of body and mind.

What strikes me as so marvellous in these cases is, the little sober reflection that seems to be bestowed upon them. The very intensity of the pain, and its long continuance, even without the aid of sudden changes, (which always occur,) ought to suggest to the mind the cause and character of the disorder: but no; in nineteen out of twenty cases, organic disease is regarded as the cause; whereas mere shadows alone impose upon the eye, and delude the judgment.

Sir C. Bell, in the Appendix to his papers on the Nerves, published in the Philosophical Transactions, has incidentally turned his attention to this subject; alluding to several cases in which he was consulted, which were clearly Hysterical. Thus he speaks of a young lady, who had a convulsive barking noise, like a cough, except that the larynx was alone affected; and there was no conforming action in the pharynx, velum, and lips. It ceased during sleep, but the moment she awoke, the family heard the unpleasant hard bark, intolerable from repetition. It continued a month, and returned three successive winters.

Sir Charles adds the following remarks: "All the subjects of these odd cases, which we do not understand, get well. This is consolatory to the patient, but not very satisfactory to ourselves. Ought it not to be a question, what nervous affections are consequent on trivial irritation? Without entering on the question, whether deranged health be followed by the imperfect and deranged action of the uterine system, or whether the latter be the primary disorder,—the *ovaria are the seat of irritation;* and the consequences are exhibited through the most susceptible system of nerves,—the respiratory system. Hence the disorder of the stomach, the spasms, globus, difficulty of deglutition, the aphonia: hence the affection of the countenance, the tears, the sobbing, and spasms of the eyes, and face, and throat, and chest, and stomach."

Such are, briefly, the opinions of Sir Charles Bell upon this subject; than whom, *quoad hoc,* no man living is entitled to more respectful attention. There can be no rational doubt, as he observes, that the nerves are the medium through which these effects of uterine irritation become developed, and so infinitely varied: and in the particular species of case which he has described, the respiratory (which, be it remembered, is not only the most susceptible, but the most comprehensive) system of nerves was principally, if not solely, inculpated. But these are not the only nerves that sympathize with uterine irritation, as evinced by these strange exhibitions; for the numerous cases before related amply testify that no single system escapes; nor is there any organ, or function of an organ, that may not be thrown into irregular and unnatural action, in consequence of primary irritation in the uterine system. It has been remarked, over and over again, that when menstruation is unnaturally suspended, or seriously defective, the spinal marrow is, in the great majority of cases, tenderly alive to pressure of the finger, as well as to the application of heat, in one or more parts of its progress; and that, when Hysterical symptoms supervene, this spinal tenderness, in ninety-nine cases out of a hundred, may be readily detected.

This structure, then, is the part first associated with uterine irritation of this description; and it is easy to conceive that, through its extensive connexions by means of the par vagum and great sympathetic nerves, every other system, and every other function of body and of mind, may be involved in disturbance and abuse.

In asserting confidently, that the ovaria are the source of irritation in these Hysterical affections, Sir Charles Bell appears to have entirely overlooked the faulty state of the uterus itself, as shown in the non-performance or mal-performance of menstruation; a circumstance, the concurrence of which, with these disorders, he himself sets forth in the very same passage. If, then, the menses be a secretion from the uterus, as generally admitted, and, indeed, proved by the observation of Dr. Hunter and others, it seems more logical, as well as more natural, to conclude the uterus itself to be the source of irritation, in which there are manifest signs of disorder during life, than the ovaria, in which there are, during life, no signs of disorder; and the detection of such must be necessarily difficult, if not impracticable. It is most probable, however, that the uterus and ovaria are simultaneously deranged.

From attentive observation, it may be inferred, that in these anomalous affections the irritation in the uterine organs is, for the most part, the primary cause of a departure from health : whilst, on the other hand, it may happen that the general health is originally impaired, the uterine functions becoming incidentally disturbed, and forming a part of the universal disorder.

It has been presumed by some writers, somewhat precipitately, that there is generally some cause of mental inquietude lurking at the bottom of an Hysterical attack, of whatever description it may be. If this opinion were properly sifted, it would be found, that the disorder of the animal functions precedes and occasions the mental despondency ; and that the latter arises in consequence of the mind being morbidly susceptible of impressions of a painful kind, magnifying every little grievance into an overwhelming misfortune, and sinking under the effect of such vexations as, in a state of sound bodily health, would not have disturbed its serenity. It is much easier to conceive this to be the case, than to imagine the dreadful sufferings with which Hysteria is sometimes connected, to take their rise from a lover's caprice or a frustrated elopement. We know very well how ready some young ladies are to be thought persons of high sensibility, and on that account consider themselves entitled to a large share of sympathy. When one of these has been lingering on under an unsuccessful treatment, month after month, it is frequently put to her, with a sagacious, penetrating look, whether "she has not something on her mind?" At first, she invariably answers in the negative, and generally, in so answering, speaks the truth. But as soon as she is left alone, she sets about a reminiscence of all the grievances she has incurred, the tears she has shed, and the trials she has passed, within the last twelve months; in which she is materially assisted by the ingenious memory of her silly companions. At last, some petty disappointment, or the death of some friend, far or near, is fixed upon, as having been a *severe shock*, and "*hinc illæ lachrymæ*:" the cause of the young lady's singular antics, and of her various forms of illness, is settled at once. There is, perhaps, no absolute mischief resulting from suffering people to impose this belief upon themselves, but it is quite another thing to impose it upon *us*. If the bodily disorder be consecutive to the depression of spirits, love of solitude, and frequent indulgence in tears, which so often characterize an Hysterical tendency, how happens it that these are dissipated by medicinal agency, and that they are removed when the bodily health is repaired? Who has not seen many a young lady in such a condition, roused to her usual activity by the brisk action of cathartics? and who has ever seen one cured by mental remedies? If we are observant of men in melancholia, or hypochondriasis, or dyspepsia, we see their minds clouded and bowed down, as if labouring under the weight of some heavy calamity; when, if they have any cause of affliction, it is such as in vigorous health would have had no such power to overwhelm or even oppress the mind, as in a state of disease. I do not mean to say that moral feelings never occasion what is called disorder of the digestive organs;—far from it; but in nineteen cases out of twenty, the dyspeptic symptoms precede the nervous ones:—and so it is in Hysteria, wherein there is always in the first instance some observable functional disturbance of the uterus. It does not, therefore, seem either reasonable or necessary to allow, that Hysteria is generated by mental shocks and disquietudes, in any other way than indirectly through that organ.

It has been before remarked that no attempt will be made in this place to explain the precise nature of the disorder of the spinal marrow and its *meninges* in Hysteria: for, in the first place, no opportunity of *post mortem* investigation has occurred to me; and, if it had, my knowledge of the nervous system and sympathies is not so much more minute and accurate than that of others as to warrant me in pretending to attach to these remarks an account of the various nervous communications, through which the Hysterical manifestations have their being. Certain I feel, that, were these disorders to be profoundly investigated by such extensive anatomical research as perhaps is only practicable in a London Hospital, much light would be thrown upon them; that Hysteria would be proved to have "a local habitation;" and that although its exhibitions sometimes "come like shadows, so depart," they never do occur without a combined error in the nervous system and in the uterine functions. All hypothesis further than this, appears to be at present unsatisfactory, and may be fallacious.

It would be no discredit to such men as Bell and Brodie, to dedicate their enterprising talents to this inquiry; and, by exploring the nature of the derangement of the nervous system in Hysteria, and tracing it to its source, they might add to their already well-earned laurels, and another valuable discovery to those for which we are already their debtors. It is a subject abounding with interest; its peculiarities and startling mutations are daily perplexing us: we marvel at the caprices of our own nature, yet years roll on, and we make no attempt to arrive at the source of these things, or to ascertain the channels through which they flow. For this undertaking, a minute knowledge of the anatomy and physiology of the nervous system must be premised; then, by extending our observations on the disorders themselves, and afterwards by noting the correspondence that may exist between the internal disturbance and the outward and visible phenomena, we may be enabled to draw such inferences as would lead, at last, to a correct theory, not only with regard to the source, but all the ramifications of this eccentric disorder. We might thus direct a suitable treatment, upon demonstrable as well as upon practical principles.

In the absence of such principles, we must make the best use we can of the evidences that are already available. Therefore, in cases where doubts arise, let the countenance be noticed; let the seat and kind of pain be described; let the state of the catamenia be inquired into; let the dorsal region of the spine be examined; and these, in conjunction with other symptoms that have been before enumerated, will form too plain a case to be misinterpreted. If I may be allowed to judge from what I am daily witnessing, I am not overrating the number, in saying, that by attention to these simple directions the health of thousands of young females may be preserved, whose constitutions are now broken down, and irreparably destroyed, by reckless and undiscriminating measures.

CPSIA information can be obtained
at www.ICGtesting.com
Printed in the USA
LVHW031313210223
739960LV00008B/853

9 783375 144029